P9-DBM-786

NO LONGER PROPERTY OF
RICHMOND HEIGHTS
MEMORIAL LIBRARY

RICHMOND HEIGHTS MEMORIAL LIBRARY
7441 Dale Avenue
Richmond Heights, MO 63117
Phone: 645-6202

Hours Open:
Monday-Thursday 9:00 A.M. - 9:00 P.M.
Friday-Saturday 9:00 A.M. - 5:00 P.M.

JUN          2000

# STOCKINGS OF BUTTERMILK

RICHMOND HEIGHTS
MEMORIAL LIBRARY
7441 DALE AVENUE
RICHMOND HEIGHTS, MO 63117

# STOCKINGS OF BUTTERMILK

## American Folktales

Edited by Neil Philip

*Illustrated by Jacqueline Mair*

CLARION BOOKS

New York

Clarion Books
a Houghton Mifflin Company imprint
215 Park Avenue South, New York, NY 10003

Published in the United States in 1999 by arrangement with
The Albion Press Ltd, Spring Hill, Idbury, Oxfordshire OX7 6RU, England

Volume copyright © 1999 The Albion Press Ltd
Illustrations copyright © 1999 Jacqueline Mair
Selection and retellings © 1999 Neil Philip
For copyright in source stories, see the Acknowledgments on p. 124

All rights reserved

For information about permission to reproduce selections from this book
write to Permissions, Houghton Mifflin Company, 215 Park Avenue South,
New York, NY 10003

Library of Congress Cataloging-in-Publication Data

Stockings of buttermilk : American folktales / edited by Neil Philip ;
    illustrated by Jacqueline Mair.
        p.   cm.
    Includes bibliographical references.
    ISBN 0–395–84980–2
    1.   Tales—United States.      I.   Philip, Neil.
GR105.S73    1999
398.2'0973—dc21                                                                98–54366
                                                                                      CIP


Typesetting: York House Typographic, London
Color origination: Culver Graphics, High Wycombe
Printing in Hong Kong/China by South China Printing Co.

1 3 5 7 9 10 8 6 4 2

For Douglas, Daralice, Leslie, John,
and Laura Boles with love

N.P.


For Lynn Cannici with love

J.M.

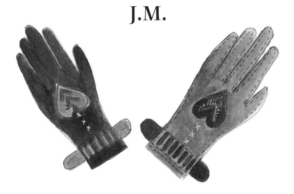

# CONTENTS

*Introduction*   13

A Stepchild That Was Treated Mighty Bad   *Kentucky*   17

The Two Witches   *New Mexico*   27

Lady Featherflight   *Massachusetts*   30

No Estiendo   *Texas*   45

King Peacock   *Louisiana*   47

Cold Feet and the Lonesome Queen   *Kentucky*   51

The Friendly Demon   *Alabama*   56

The Little Bull with the Golden Horns   *Missouri*   62

The Gold in the Chimney   *Kentucky*   73

Three Eileschpijjel Stories   *Pennsylvania*   78

Jack and the Beanstalk   *Kentucky*   81

The Big Cabbage   *Michigan*   87

Tobe Killed a Bear   *Missouri*   88

The Cat That Went a-Traveling   *Kentucky*   91

The Enchanted Prince   *New Mexico*   95

Miss Liza and the King   *Georgia*   104

*Notes on the Stories*   113

*Further Reading*   122

*Acknowledgments*   124

# INTRODUCTION

Everyone knows the French fairy tales of Charles Perrault: "Cinderella," "Sleeping Beauty," "Little Red Riding Hood." Everyone knows the German household tales of the Brothers Grimm: "The Frog Prince," "Rumpelstiltskin," "Snow White." Those with an interest in folk and fairy tales may be aware that these stories can be found in different versions in many different cultures. But many readers may be surprised to find such stories in authentic American dress.

The tales came to these shores from elsewhere, of course, brought as household goods by each generation of settlers. But stories, like plants, can naturalize fast. In 1923, for instance, folklorist Elsie Clews Parsons published two volumes of *Folk-Lore from the Cape Verde Islands,* collected in Portuguese Creole along the eastern seaboard. In just two generations, the traditional hero of these tales, Pedr' Quadrad, had begun to settle in nicely. He meets enchanted princesses "even prettier than Americans," to whom he gives apples so sweet, "you could smell them from here to California."

America's store of folktales is vast, so hard choices had to be made about what to include in this book. I have concentrated on stories from the European cultures that had the earliest shaping influence on the new country: those of England, Scotland, and Ireland; France; Spain; Germany. It would have been just as easy to fill the book with stories from Italian, or Armenian, or Portuguese, or Greek, or Eastern European, or Scandinavian sources; to trace the impact of the African story tradition; or to invite the reader into the worlds of Chinese, Japanese, or Korean folklore as they have developed in their new home. Each of these has added a distinctive spice to the American folktale.

There was, of course, already a rich storytelling culture in America, that of the Native Americans. But while Native Americans quickly began to tell stories from the Indo-European tradition (some of which can be sampled in Stith Thompson's *Tales of the North American Indians*), the reverse does not apply, and Native American storytelling remains a distinct tradition best explored at more depth than would have been possible here.

The American storytelling voice has a characteristic bounce and vitality. These features were already strongly present by the early nineteenth century, as folklorist Ralph S. Boggs showed in a 1934 study of "North Carolina Folktales Current in the 1820's" in the *Journal of American Folk-Lore*.

An Ozark version of "The Frog Prince," collected by the indefatigable Vance Randolph, begins: "One time there was a pretty girl walking down the street, and she heard somebody say, 'Hi, Toots!' But when she looked around there was nobody in sight, just a little old toad-frog setting on the sidewalk." Compare that with the Brothers Grimm, in a standard English translation: "In olden times, when wishing still helped one, there lived a king whose daughters were all beautiful, but the youngest was so beautiful that the sun itself, which has seen so much, was astonished whenever it shone in her face."

I hope that the stories in this book will retain on the page some of the freshness and informality, the beautiful direct- ness, of the spoken stories that lie behind them. Some of the stories will seem familiar—versions of "Jack and the Bean- stalk," "Snow White," "Aladdin"—while others may seem new and strange. But each, for me, has that haunting quality of a tune first heard in a dream.

All of these tunes, and many more that I found no room for, would be played on the fiddle at the grand weddings that end so many of these stories. And, in the words of one traditional Irish-American story ending, all who go to those weddings will get fine presents—"shoes of paper and stockings of but- termilk."

> I stepped on a piece of tin,
> The tin bended,
> My story ended.

NEIL PHILIP

RICHMOND HEIGHTS
MEMORIAL LIBRARY
1441 DALE AVENUE
RICHMOND HEIGHTS, MO 63117

# A STEPCHILD THAT WAS TREATED MIGHTY BAD

## Kentucky

Hearing some women talking about a man over at Vest marrying again and pondering with them on how his new woman will treat her stepchild, his pretty, little girl, put me in mind of an olden tale about a stepchild that was treated mighty bad. Set down and rest yourself a little minute while I tell.

They was a man and a woman, not nobody you ever heard tell of, way back in time. Everybody has done forgot their names. A king and a queen they are said to have been, anyhow that's what I always heard tell. They had an onliest child, a girl it was, and pretty as a picture; and good, too, I reckon. They named her Snow White and Rose Red, on account of her skin was white as snow in wintertime and her cheeks were red like blooms on the rosebushes in the summertime.

The way some folks tell the tale, the mother died when she birthed little Snow White. Some tells that she had a fever. I don't know; anyhow, she died, and left her man and the baby. On her deathbed she made her man promise not to marry again and bring no stepmother to be mean to Snow White. He made promise, and I don't misdoubt he aimed at the time to do like he promised. But he had to hire somebody to do the

17

needful things for his child that it takes a woman to do anyways right.

Well, the nurse-woman was a clever person, and not bad-looking, neither. She made little Snow White like her and acted real motherly and nice. The man took notice how good she tended Snow White. Then he started to notice she weren't bad-looking. First thing you know, he was a-courting her—just what she had in her mind from the first minute she hired herself out to take care of Snow White for him. Pretty soon he named marrying, the promise he made to his dead wife gone clean out of his mind. The nurse-woman jumped at the chance, and so they got married and she moved her house plunder to his house and rented out her place for cash money.

When Snow White got to be of an age to be noticed for being pretty in a way to make womenfolks jealous of her, her stepmother turned poison mean. She wanted to be the best-looking woman in the neighborhood, and she treated pretty girls like poison, more especially her stepchild that was far and away the prettiest girl that ever lived in the neighborhood.

The stepmother had a looking glass hung up on her wall, and she loved to look at herself in it and think how pretty. It made her so mad to see how her stepchild was better favored in looks than she was her ownself that she couldn't hardly stand it. She would stand there and sass her looking glass for not making her look pretty all the time. Some tells how the looking glass sassed her back and always told her Snow White was far and away the prettiest. I don't never tell it that-a-way, for I ain't got no faith in a looking glass that talks.

This mean-hearted woman thought up ways to get rid of Snow White. She said one day to a strange man going by with a gun and a hound-dog like he was going to hunt in the woods, "I'll give you six bits, maybe a dollar, if you will toll this girl off in the woods a far piece and leave her there to perish. I purely can't stand the sight of her any longer." He wouldn't promise till she gave him ten dollars and six bits, all the cash money she had. Then he tolled the girl off, telling her he could show her fine places to pick flower blooms in the woods.

Once he got her way back in the deep woods, a far piece from home, he slipped off and left her picking wild flower blooms. But his hound-dog stayed with her, close by to be a protection. So the man had ten dollars and six bits in his pockets for doing a mean-hearted thing; but he lost a good hunting dog, though I don't know how much it woulda been worth.

Come night, the hound-dog led her to a little house he had found, and it had beds and things in it. The dog went off somewhere, and Snow White flew busy and cooked up a good supper. She waited for somebody to come and eat what she cooked; but when they never came, she had as much as she wanted for supper and put the rest of the supper in the cupboard in the cook room.

Seven rocking chairs she found in the house, and she rocked as much as she wanted to till she felt rested. Then she found seven beds, all made up smooth and nice but one. It was all rumpled up, and she smoothed out the covers and fixed it nice. Then she laid down and went to sleep.

Seven little men came home from their day's work chopping trees in the woods. Rummaging in the cupboard, they found what Snow White cooked; and they washed their hands and had a good supper. They rocked a while to rest from the hard day's work, and then they got sleepy. They went upstairs to the room with their beds all in a row, and they found Snow White. They tipped around, being quiet, and didn't wake her up at all. One of the little men slept on a pallet bed on the floor so Snow White could sleep on his good soft bed.

Come morning, they made their manners to Snow White, and they asked her to be a sister to them and keep their house tidy and cook and sew, and they would make her a good living, and they would dearly love to have her for their sister. The hound-dog came back and stayed with her in the daytime to be a protection while the little men chopped in the woods. Of nights the dog would go off somewheres.

After a time the mean-hearted stepmother found out that Snow White was still living and getting prettier every day of her life. So the stepmother fixed herself up so Snow White wouldn't know her and went to the little house in the woods where Snow White lived with the little men. And the hound-dog barked and raised his bristles, but she looked just like an old woman peddling things around the country. And Snow White made the hound-dog hush up and lay down.

The stepmother had a golden comb that she gave to Snow White. When she put it in Snow White's hair, she fell down like dead, for the comb had poison in it. Then the old woman went off.

The dog went and fetched the little men to come see about Snow White. They pulled the poison comb out of her hair and she got right up and cooked supper. They told her not to let no strangers come in the house when they went off to their job of work.

Another time the mean-hearted stepmother found out Snow White had come alive. She had to think up a new way to get shut of her. She put some poison on a finger ring and sent it to Snow White. I don't know how, maybe by a neighbor passing through. Anyhow, the finger ring made Snow White fall down like dead. The hound-dog went and fetched the little men from their job of work, and they pulled off the finger ring, and Snow White got up and cooked supper.

The last time it was some fine apples the mean-hearted stepmother sent to Snow White. The finest red apple had

poison in it, and Snow White had scarce swallowed ary bite till she fell down like dead with a piece of apple in her mouth. That time the hound went and fetched the little men, but they didn't see nothing to pull off of her to make her come to. So they had to give her up for dead. They laid her out in a coffin with glass so they could look at her. They fixed flower blossoms fresh around the coffin every day after they put it in a church up on a mountain. The hound-dog stayed by it to guard it from harm.

One day a fine man, maybe a king, came along and looked through the glass coffin at Snow White. The hound-dog liked the man and let him look. The man loved Snow White and wanted to have her with him. When the little men came home from work, he talked and coaxed till they let him carry Snow White in her glass coffin home with him to his big fine house. Going down the mountain, he dropped the coffin, though he didn't aim to. Being dropped jarred the piece of apple out of Snow White's mouth, and she came alive again. They went back to the little house and told the little men about it, and they let Snow White marry him and go to live in his big fine house.

At his house she didn't have to cook and keep house, so she took the hound-dog for protection and went a-walking about the place. Some old apple trees were all bowed down and about to break. They begged her to shake their limbs and make some of the apples fall off so they wouldn't break. And she was glad to do it. Then some cows asked her would she milk out their bags so they wouldn't get all sore. And she was glad to do it. Then she came to an old woman with a heavy basket. And she was more than glad to carry the old woman's basket, not even waiting to get asked. I reckon the old woman went home with her and stayed all night. Anyhow, in the morning the old woman said to her, "You can keep that old basket to pay back your trouble."

When the old woman had gone off, Snow White opened up the lid of the basket, and it was full of all kinds of fine clothes made of gold and jewels besides a heap of other pretties more than just clothes to wear.

Snow White dressed up fine and her man thought she was mighty pretty. Then they went to visit her daddy, and they took the old woman's basket full of things, for the more Snow White took fine things out, the more the basket got full of things again. And she filled her daddy's pockets up full of gold money and made him a present of some more golden things. And she even made a present to her mean-hearted step-mother.

And the mean-hearted stepmother tried to steal the basket away from Snow White. But when she took hold of it, the basket got so heavy she couldn't lift it or even budge it one bit, and couldn't take anything out of it neither.

So after Snow White went back home, with her man a-carrying her fine basket, the mean-hearted stepmother took it in her head to do just like Snow White, and get her a fine basket of golden money and things to wear and jewels and other pretties.

She walked through the woods to the house where the seven little men lived. They were off at work, but she never turned her hand to do a thing about the place. She just sat down and rocked all day till she broke down all the rocking chairs and left the pieces piled up in a heap. Then she laid down to sleep and rumpled up all the beds. The little men ran her off and wouldn't put up with her at all.

She walked around in the woods hunting a place to stay all night, and I don't know if she found any place or how she

made out. I reckon I just forgot that part.

Anyhow, come morning, she met up with the apple trees that had too many apples again, for what Snow White left on the trees had got bigger and heavier. The orchard trees asked the mean-hearted stepmother would she shake their limbs and make some of the apples fall off so they wouldn't break, and she said she never aimed to do no hard work, and she walked on.

The cows asked her would she milk out their bags so they wouldn't get all sore. But she wouldn't do that neither.

She kept on walking and looking for the old woman with the basket full of fine things. After a time she found the old woman setting down to rest. The mean-hearted old stepmother never even said, "Howdy." She just grabbed up the basket and ran off as fast as she could. Whenever she got home, she opened up the basket quick as she could and made

25

a grab. She nearly fell down dead in a fright when she saw what she grabbed—a handful of snakes and toad-frogs. She flung them away in the weeds and tried to empty out the basket. But it stayed full to the brim with toad-frogs and snakes, full of poison and mean as could be.

When her man saw what she had fetched home that he couldn't get rid of, he left her and went to live with Snow White and her man in his big fine house.

The mean-hearted step-mother got killed to be rid of her meanness but I don't know how she got killed. And it don't make me no difference.

# THE TWO WITCHES

## New Mexico

One time there were two male witches, a good witch and a bad witch, and they made a bet. This was a long time ago.

They said they would change themselves into horses and run a race. The witch who lost the race would have to stay a horse for all time.

So they ran the race, and the good witch lost, and he had to stay a horse because of the bet.

So the bad witch took the horse and sold him to a man. But he said, "Don't ever take the halter off of this horse. If you do, too bad."

Now one day a little boy took the horse down to the river for water, and a priest came by. The priest said, "Why are you watering that horse with the halter on? The horse can't drink. Take off the halter." So the boy took off the halter, and the horse changed right away into a little fish.

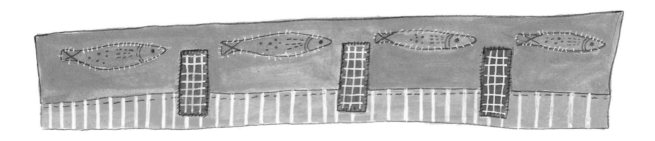

Now that bad witch was flying around as a hawk, and he saw what happened. So he changed himself into a big fish.

The little fish saw this, and changed into a bird.

The bad witch changed back into a hawk and chased the bird.

The little bird flew and flew, until he was too tired. He saw a princess in a garden, and flew down to that princess and hid in her lap. She took that poor little bird and put it in a cage. No one could get him now. He was so happy, that bird, he sang all day long.

But the princess wasn't happy. She took sick, and was sad all the time and never laughed. The bad witch then changed into a doctor, and he came along and said he could cure her, but he would need the blood of that bird.

So the king gave him the bird, and he cut its throat. But when the blood ran out, instead of blood it was seed corn.

The bad witch changed into a hen, and ate up the seed; but he couldn't find the last seed. And the last seed changed into a coyote and ate up that hen!

And then the coyote changed back into a man, and married the princess.

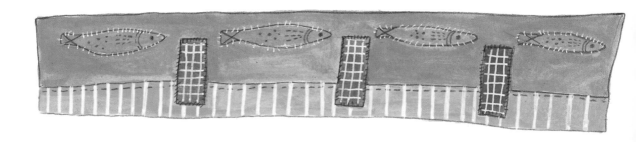

# LADY FEATHERFLIGHT

## Massachusetts

A poor woman, living on the edge of a wood, found nothing in the cupboard for the next day's breakfast. She called her boy, Reuben, and said, "You must now go into the wide world, for if you stay here there will be two of us to starve. I have nothing for you but this piece of black bread. On the other side of the forest lies the world. Find your way to it, and earn your living honestly." She bade him goodbye, and he started on his way.

He knew his way some distance out into the blackest part of the forest, for he had often gone there for logs. But after walking all day he lost the path, and knew that he was lost. Still he traveled on and on, as long as daylight lasted, and then lay down and slept.

The next morning he ate his black bread and walked on all day. At night he saw lights before him and was guided by them to a large palace. At last the door was opened, and a lovely lady appeared. She said as she saw him, "Go away as quickly as you can. My father will soon come home, and he will surely eat you."

Reuben said, "Can't you hide me and give me something to eat? Otherwise I shall fall dead at your door." At first she refused, but then she yielded to Reuben's pleas and told him to come in and hide behind the oven. Then she gave him food

and told him that her father was a giant who ate men and women. But perhaps he could stay overnight, as she already had supper prepared.

After a while, the giant came banging at the door, shouting, "Featherflight, let me in, let me in." As she opened the door, he came in, saying, "Where have you stowed the man? I smelt him all the way through that wood."

Featherflight said, "Oh, Father, he is nothing but a poor little thin boy. He would make but half a mouthful, and his bones would stick in your throat. And besides, he wants to work for you; perhaps you can make him useful. But sit down to supper now, and after supper I will show him to you."

So she set before him half of a fat heifer, a sheep, and a turkey, which he swallowed so fast that his hair stood on end. When he had finished, Featherflight beckoned to Reuben, who came trembling from behind the oven. The giant looked at him scornfully and said, "Indeed, as you say, he is but half a mouthful. But there is room for flesh there, and we must fatten him up for a few days. Meanwhile, he must earn his vittles. See here, my young snip, can you do a day's work in a day?"

And Reuben answered bravely, "I can do a day's work in a day as well as another."

So the giant said, "Well, go to bed now. I will tell you what to do in the morning."

So Reuben went to bed, and the giant lay down on the floor with his head in Featherflight's lap, and she combed his hair and brushed it until he was fast asleep.

The next morning Reuben was called bright and early and was taken out to the farmyard, where stood a large barn that had lost its roof in a storm. Here the giant stopped and said, "Behind this barn you will find a hill of feathers. Thatch me this barn with them, and earn your supper; and look you, if it is not done when I come back tonight, you shall be fried in bread crumbs and eaten whole for supper." Then he left, laughing to himself as he went down the road.

Reuben went bravely to work and found a ladder and a basket. He filled the basket, ran up the ladder, and then tried hard to make a beginning on the thatched roof. But as soon as he got a handful of feathers in place, half of them would fly away before he could weave them in. He tried for hours without success, until half of the hill of feathers was scattered to the four winds, and he had not finished a hand's breadth of roof. Then he sat down at the foot of the ladder and began to cry.

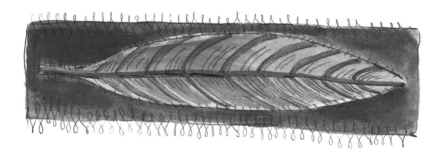

Out came Lady Featherflight with a basket on her arm, saying, "Eat now, and cry later. Meanwhile, I will try to think what I can do to help you." Reuben felt cheered and began to eat while Featherflight walked round the barn, singing as she went:

> Birds of land and birds of sea,
> Come and thatch this roof for me.

As she walked round the second time, the sky grew dark, and a heavy cloud hid the sun. It came nearer and nearer to the earth, separating at last into hundreds and thousands of birds. Each, as it flew, dropped a feather on the roof and tucked it neatly in; and when Reuben's meal was finished, the thatch was finished too.

Then Featherflight said, "Let us talk and enjoy ourselves until my father the giant comes home." So they wandered round the grounds and the stables, and Lady Featherflight told Reuben about all the treasure in the strong room, while Reuben told Lady Featherflight how he had been born without a cent.

Soon they went back to the house, and Reuben helped while Featherflight prepared supper, which tonight was four-teen loaves of bread, two sheep, and a jack-pudding to finish, which would have almost filled the little house where Reuben was born.

Soon the giant came home, thundered at the door again, and shouted, "Let me in! Let me in!" Featherflight served him with the supper, and the giant ate it with great relish. As soon as he had finished, he called to Reuben and asked him about his work. Reuben said, "I told you I could do a day's work in a day as well as another. You'll have no fault to find." The giant said nothing, and Reuben went to bed. Then, as before, the giant lay down on the floor with his head in Featherflight's lap. She combed his hair and brushed his head till he fell fast asleep.

The next morning the giant called Reuben into the yard and looked at his day's work. All he said was, "This is not your doing." Then he pointed to a heap of seed, nearly as high as the barn, saying, "Here is your day's work. Separate the seeds, each kind into its own pile. Let it be done when I come home tonight, or you shall be fried in bread crumbs and I shall swallow you, bones and all." Then the giant went off down the road, laughing as he went.

Reuben seated himself by the heap, took a handful of seeds, and began to put corn in one pile, rye in another, oats in another, and so on. He had not even come to the end of all the different kinds when noon came, and the sun was right overhead. The heap was no smaller, and Reuben was tired out. So he sat down, hugged his knees, and cried.

Out came Featherflight with a basket on her arm, which she set down before Reuben, saying, "Eat now, and cry later." So Reuben ate with a will while Lady Featherflight walked round and round the heap, singing as she went:

> Insects that crawl and insects that fly,
> Come and sort this seed for me.

As she walked round the heap for the second time, still singing, the ground about her looked as if it was moving. From behind each grain of sand, each daisy stem, each blade of grass, there came some little insect, gray, black, brown, or green, and began to work at the seeds. Each chose out one kind and made a great heap by itself.

By the time Reuben had finished his meal, the great heap was divided into countless others, and Reuben and Feather-flight could walk and talk to their heart's content for the rest of the day.

As the sun went down, the giant came home, thundered at the door again, and shouted, "Let me in! Let me in!"

Featherflight greeted him with his supper, already laid, and he sat down and ate, with a great appetite, four fat pigs, three fat pullets, and an old gander, finishing off with a jack-pudding. Then he was so sleepy he could not keep his head up. All he said was, "Go to bed, youngster! I'll see your work

tomorrow." Then, as before, the giant laid himself down on the floor with his head in Featherflight's lap. She combed his hair and brushed it until he fell fast asleep.

The next morning the giant called Reuben into the farm-yard earlier than before. "It is but fair to call you early, for I have work for you, more than a strong man can do." He showed him a heap of sand, saying, "Make me a rope to tether my herd of cows, so that they may not leave their stalls before milking time." Then he turned on his heel and went down the road laughing.

Reuben took some sand in his hands, gave one twist, threw it down, went to the door, and called out, "Featherflight, Featherflight, this is beyond even you! I feel myself already rolled in bread crumbs and swallowed, bones and all!"

Out came Featherflight, saying brightly, "It's not so bad as all that. Sit down, and we will plan what to do."

They talked and planned all day. Just before the giant came home, they went to the top of the stairs to Reuben's room; then Featherflight pricked Reuben's finger and dropped a drop of blood on each of the three stairs. Then she came down and prepared the supper, which tonight was a brace of turkeys, three fat geese, five fat hens, six fat pigeons, seven fat woodcocks, and half a score of quail, with a jack-pudding.

When he had finished, the giant turned to Featherflight with a growl, saying, "Why are you so mean with the food tonight? Is there nothing else in the larder? This boy whets my appetite." He turned to Reuben. "It will be well for you, young sir, if you have done your work. Is it done?"

"No, sir," said Reuben boldly. "I said I could do a day's work in a day as well as another, but no better."

The giant said, "Featherflight, prick him for me with a larding needle, hang him in the chimney corner well wrapped

in bacon, and serve him to me tomorrow for my breakfast."

"Yes, Father," said Featherflight.

Then, as before, the giant laid himself down on the floor with his head in Featherflight's lap. She combed his hair and brushed his head, and he fell fast asleep.

Reuben went to bed in his room at the top of the stairs. As soon as the giant was snoring, Featherflight called to Reuben softly, saying, "I have the keys of the treasure house; come with me." They opened the treasure house and took out bags of gold and silver. Then they untied the halter of the best horse from the best stall in the best stable.

Reuben mounted, with Featherflight behind, and off they went.

At three o'clock in the morning, forgetting his orders of the night before, the giant wakened, turned over, and said, "Reuben, get up."

"Yes, sir," said the first drop of blood.

At four o'clock the giant wakened and said, "Reuben, get up."

"Yes, sir," said the second drop of blood.

At five o'clock the giant turned over and said, "Reuben, get up."

"Yes, sir," said the third drop of blood.

At six o'clock the giant wakened, turned over, and said, "Reuben, get up!"

But this time there was no answer.

Then in a great fury the giant said, "Featherflight has overslept—my breakfast won't be ready." He rushed up to Featherflight's room; it was empty. He dashed downstairs to the chimney corner, to see if Reuben was still hanging there, but found neither Reuben nor Lady Featherflight.

"They have run away!" he said. "I must get my seven-league boots from the treasure house." He looked under his pillow for the key, but it was gone. He rushed down and found the door of the strong-room wide open, and the bags of gold and silver gone. He looked in the stables and found the best horse from the best stall in the best stable gone too.

The giant tugged on his seven-league boots and went after them swifter than the wind. The runaways had been galloping for several hours when Reuben heard a sound behind them and, turning, saw the giant in the distance. "Oh, Featherflight, Featherflight, all is lost!"

But Featherflight said, "Keep steady, Reuben. Look in the horse's right ear, and throw behind you over your right shoulder whatever you find."

Reuben looked, and found a little stick of wood. He threw it over his right shoulder, and there grew up behind them a huge forest of hardwood.

"We are saved," said Reuben.

"Not so certain," said Lady Featherflight, "but we have gained some time. Urge on the horse."

The giant could not get through the wood, but he went back for an ax, and soon hacked and hewed his way through and was on their trail again.

Reuben again heard a sound, turned and saw the giant, and said to Lady Featherflight, "All is lost!"

"Keep steady, Reuben," said Featherflight. "Look in the horse's left ear, and throw over your left shoulder whatever you find."

Reuben looked, and found a single drop of water. He threw

it over his left shoulder, and there arose a great lake of water.

The giant stopped on the other side, and shouted, "How did you get through?"

"We drank our way through," Featherflight replied.

The giant laughed scornfully. "Anything you can do, I can do," he said. He threw himself down at the water's edge and drank, and drank, and drank, and then he burst.

Now Reuben and Featherflight could ride on quietly, until they came near to a town. Here they stopped, and Reuben said, "Climb this tree, and hide in the branches till I come

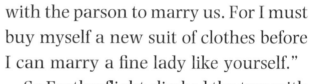

with the parson to marry us. For I must buy myself a new suit of clothes before I can marry a fine lady like yourself."

So Featherflight climbed the tree with the thickest branches she could find and waited there, looking down between the leaves into a spring below.

Now, this spring was used by all the wives of the town to draw water for breakfast. No water was so sweet anywhere else; and early in the morning they all came with pitchers and pails for a gossip, and to draw water for the kettle.

The first who came was the carpenter's wife, and as she bent over the clear spring she saw, not herself, but Featherflight's lovely face reflected in the water. She looked at it with astonishment and cried, "What? I, stay a carpenter's wife, when I am so handsome? No, I won't!" And she threw down her pitcher, and off she went.

The next who came was the potter's wife, and as she bent over the clear spring, she saw, not herself, but Featherflight's lovely face reflected in the water. She looked at it with astonishment and cried, "What? I, stay a potter's wife, when I am so handsome? No, I won't!" And she threw down her pitcher, and off she went.

All the wives of all the men of the town came in turn, and each of them, seeing Featherflight's reflection, mistook it for her own, threw down her pitcher, and set off to make her face her fortune.

All the men of the town began to want their breakfast, and, one after another, each went out into the marketplace to ask if anyone had seen his wife. Each came with the same question, and all received the same answer. All the wives had been seen going to the spring, but none returning from it.

The men began to fear foul play, and all together walked out to the spring. When they reached it, they found the broken pitchers scattered all over the grass and the pails, bottom upward, floating on the water.

One of them, looking over the edge, saw the face reflected and, knowing it was not his own, looked up. Seeing Lady Featherflight, he called to his comrades, "Here is the enchantress who has bewitched our wives. Let's kill her." And they dragged her out of the tree, in spite of all she could say.

Just at that moment Reuben came galloping up on his horse, with the parson behind. You would never guess the fine gentleman to be the poor ragged boy who had passed up the road so short a time before. He saw the crowd and shouted, "What's the matter? What are you doing to my wife?"

The parson told them to stop and let Lady Featherflight tell her own story. When she told them how their wives had mistaken her face for theirs, they were silent for a moment, and then one and all cried, "If we have married such fools, we are well rid of them!" And they walked back to town.

Then the parson married Reuben and Lady Featherflight on the spot, and blessed them with water from the spring, and then went home with them to the great house that Reuben had bought in town with the bags of gold and silver.

There the newlyweds lived happily until the money was all gone. "Why don't we go and fetch more of the giant's treasure?" said Reuben. But they could not cross the water.

"Why not build a bridge?" said Lady Featherflight, and so the bridge was built.

They went over with wagons and horses and brought back so heavy a load that the bridge broke, and the gold was lost.

Reuben lamented and said, "Now we can have no more from the giant's treasure-house."

But Featherflight said, "Keep steady, Reuben. Why not mend the bridge?"

So the bridge was mended,
And now my story's ended.

# NO ESTIENDO

## Texas

Once a Mexican and an American were grubbing stumps by the day. They camped together and decided to divide their chores. The American didn't know much Spanish; he just nodded and said *"Sí"* ("Yes") to everything the Mexican said.

When they went back to camp the first evening, the Mexican said, "We'll have *tortillas de harina* (wheat-flour tortillas) tonight." The American didn't understand a word, but he nodded and said, *"Sí."*

*"Yo amaso,"* the Mexican said. ("I will knead the dough.")

The American nodded, and said, *"Sí."*

*"Tú estiendes."* ("You roll the dough flat.")

The American pricked up his ears at that. He thought the Mexican had said, "You understand." (*"Tú entiendes."*) He shook his head and said, *"No estiendo."*

"What?" the Mexican said. "You won't do it? Why not?"

*"No estiendo,"* the American said.

"You're a stubborn one," the Mexican said. "All right, we'll switch jobs. *Tú amasas, yo estiendo."*

*"No estiendo,"* the American said.

"If you say once more that you won't do it, I'll whack you over the head with this ax handle."

"*No estiendo,*" the American said.

So the Mexican hauled back and gave the American a lick with the ax handle, and then another and another. And no matter how much he beat him, the American kept saying, "*No estiendo! No estiendo!*"

So they had no *tortillas de harina* that night.

# KING PEACOCK

## Louisiana

Once there was a lady who was pretty, so pretty that she never wanted to marry. She found something bad to say about all her suitors: "Oh, you are too ugly." "Oh, you are too small." "Oh, your mouth is too big." There was something she didn't like about everyone.

Then one day a fine gentleman came. He was in a golden carriage drawn by eight white horses. He asked the lady to marry him. She said she didn't want to. He was so angry, he said, "In a year you will give birth to a daughter who is much, much prettier than you."

The lady told him to go away. "I never want to set eyes on you again."

Well, a year later she had a pretty, pretty little girl. When she saw how pretty the child was, she shut her up in a room at the far end of the house, with a nurse to look after her.

The little girl grew up, and the bigger she got, the prettier she got. The nurse never let her leave her room. But one day, while the nurse was sweeping the floor, she left the door open, and the young girl looked outside and saw a large bird.

"Oh, Mama Tété," she said, "what is that handsome bird?"

"That, my little one, is a peacock."

"Oh, Mama Tété," she said, "if ever I get married, I want to marry King Peacock."

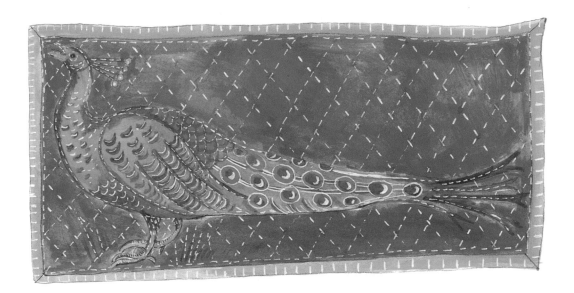

And her nurse said, "May the good Lord hear you, child."

That very day the mother came, called the nurse into a corner, and drew out from beneath her skirt a great knife, saying, "I want you to kill my daughter. She has grown prettier than I."

The nurse began to cry and beg for mercy for the poor child, but it was all in vain, for that black heart could not be softened. When night came, the nurse said to the girl, "My poor child, I must kill you; your mother wants me to."

The poor child was so good, she said, "Well, Mama Tété, do it, if it is what my mother wants."

But the nurse said, "No, I haven't got the heart to do it, my little one. Here, take these three seeds, and throw yourself into the well and drown yourself. But before you jump in the well, swallow one of the seeds, and you will not suffer a thing."

The girl thanked her nurse and went to drown herself. She walked until she came to a large well. She threw herself into it, and before she touched the water she took one of the seeds to

48

put it in her mouth. But instead of putting it in her mouth, she dropped it in the water, and at once the well dried up.

The girl was so sorry that she had not drowned. She climbed out of the well and walked and walked far into the wood, until she came to a little house. She knocked at the door, and an old woman opened it.

The old woman cried out when she saw the pretty girl there, "Oh, Lord, my child, what are you thinking of, coming here? Don't you know that my husband is an ogre? He will eat you up!"

The girl said, "Well, that is my wish, for my mother has said that I must die."

Then the old woman said, "If that is so, come in, my poor child, but it is a great pity."

The poor child sat down in a corner and cried while she waited for the ogre. All at once they heard his heavy footsteps. As soon as the door was opened, the ogre shouted, "Oh, wife, I smell fresh meat! Where is it?"

He ran toward the girl, who looked up at him with her big eyes, and then he stepped back, saying, "Oh, wife, do you think I could eat a pretty girl like this? No, I just want to keep her to look at."

The girl told him that she was tired, so he took her to a beautiful bedroom and told his wife to fan her with peacock feathers while she slept.

The girl said to herself, "It would be best for me to die now, for perhaps tomorrow the ogre will want to eat me." She took one of the seeds and put it in her mouth, and fell into a deep sleep. She slept and slept, and all the while the ogre's wife fanned her with peacock feathers.

After she had slept for three days, the ogre looked at her and said to his wife, "It is a great pity, but I think she is dead." He went to the town and bought a golden coffin. He put the girl in it and set it adrift on the river. The coffin floated away, downriver, downriver.

Far away, King Peacock was enjoying the cool breeze on the levee with all his courtiers. When he saw something shining on the river, he told the courtiers to run and see what it was. They took a skiff out onto the water. They cried, "It's a coffin," and they brought it to the king.

When he saw the pretty young girl, who seemed to be sleeping, he said, "Take her to my room." He wanted to try to awaken her.

In his room, he rubbed eau de cologne on her face, but it did no good. Then he opened her mouth to see what pretty teeth she had. He saw something red between her front teeth, so he took a golden pin and eased it out. It was the seed. As soon as it fell out, the girl opened her eyes, and said, "I am so glad to see you."

The king said, "I am King Peacock. Will you marry me?"

The girl said, "I will."

And there was a grand wedding, so grand that they told me to go and tell the story everywhere, everywhere.

# COLD FEET AND THE LONESOME QUEEN

## Kentucky

Many a time, when a person has a good solid name, he never hears nobody call him that name a dozen times in his life. That was the way with a man named John in a tale the Irishman told me one time. This here man got nicknamed Cold Feet, and that was the only name he ever did hear anybody call him by. He got that nickname from growing so fast and so big when he was still a boy that only a part of him could get into the house at one time. With his head and shoulders in the warm house and the rest of him outside in the weather, he was always complaining about his feet being cold. That was how come he got the nickname of Cold Feet, and seems like folks plumb forgot his name was John.

Naturally, a boy that big and still a-growing would eat up creation. It came to a time when his mammy just couldn't make a living for him. So he left home to seek his fortune.

He hired himself out to a knight in a castle to herd cows for a year and a day. The cows never made any trouble for Cold Feet but grazed all day peaceful as could be and went home at milking time in the evening.

Four giants lived in the same country as the knight in the castle. Every day one of them would come and threaten to do

51

Cold Feet harm lessen he left the country. He was bigger than the giants and still a-growing, and they were afraid he would damage their reputation for size. They were different from other giants, for they had lots of heads instead of just one.

The first giant had four heads, and he threatened Cold Feet with four mouths all talking loud and mean at the same time. Cold Feet got enough of his sass and up and killed him and hid his four heads under some big rocks. It was the same way for three days after that, with a giant that had six heads, then one with eight heads, and at the last a giant with a dozen heads on his shoulders and all his dozen mouths saying mean and threatening things to Cold Feet. His heads were soon off and hid under big rocks. And that was the last of the four giants.

But on the fifth day the giants' mammy came to threaten Cold Feet. She was a fearsome old hag with fingernails and toenails of steel, and each fingernail and toenail weighed seven pounds. Cold Feet was no match for her and she put him under a spell to go to the Land of the Lonesome Queen and bring back the sword of light, the loaf of bread not tasted, and the bottle of liquor that nobody ever drank from. To make it harder for Cold Feet to get these things she shrunk him down to natural size.

Cold Feet gave up his job herding cows and collected his wages and left for the Land of the Lonesome Queen. He was three days and nights on the way, and each night he stayed with a different old man, and each old man gave him a set of directions about how to get one of the things he was going after. The Irishman that told me the tale never gave me the directions. But what the old men told Cold Feet worked, and he got the sword of light, and the loaf of bread nobody ever tasted, and the bottle of liquor never drunk from.

Then he found the Lonesome Queen asleep in her castle— musta been a spell of some kind, for Cold Feet slept with her all night . . . and she never woke up at all even when he stole one of her golden garters to remember her by.

On the way home Cold Feet got cheated out of the things he had been sent after. How he got cheated I never heard tell. He was afraid to face the giants' mammy that sent him on the journey to the Land of the Lonesome Queen, so he went back to his own mammy.

Shrunk up the way he was now, he could live in the house with her; and he ate no more than any common man. He herded cows and hired out to the neighbors. He managed to make a living but had never a penny to lay by.

Enduring this time the Lonesome Queen woke up . . . and in the course of time she had a fine boy baby.

The boy looked pine-blank like Cold Feet; but the Lonesome Queen couldn't know that, for she never did see Cold Feet. When he was nearly grown, Cold Feet's boy set out to travel the world and find his pap. On his way, he got back all the things that Cold Feet had been cheated out of years before, and carried them along with him. After a time, he came to the house where Cold Feet lived, and he stopped by the spring to get a cool drink of water.

The boy's granny came to the spring to get a bucket of water and she saw that this here boy favored Cold Feet, so she asked him to go home with her to wait till Cold Feet came home from work. The Lonesome Queen had given her boy the other golden garter that she had on when Cold Feet stole one.

She told him his pap would have the garter to match. And it turned out that way.

Cold Feet took the golden garter out of his pocket and matched it with the one the Lonesome Queen's boy had. Cold Feet and the boy's granny made over him a lot, and he made them a present of the loaf of bread that nobody ever tasted, and the sword of light and the bottle of liquor never drunk. Then they all went to the Land of the Lonesome Queen, and she never was lonesome after that.

# THE FRIENDLY DEMON

## Alabama

This old man, he lived in the valley, see, and he traveled around, see, doing cobbling, see. He was a very peculiar man, see, very peculiar. People came to him for advice, see.

In a nearby city lived a lad about eighteen years of age. He started out to make his fortune, see, and he met this man, the man asked him where he was going, see. He said he was going out to make his fortune, see, on his life's journey to make his fortune.

The man said, "Follow me." The man picked up a very large stone, and told the young fellow to pick one up too, but the young fellow couldn't lift one.

So they carried the stone with them, and when they got hungry, the man said some words over the stone, and passed his hands over it, and it became a loaf of bread. He said, "Come on, sit down and eat."

When they were ready to leave, this time the boy picked up a large stone, but the man did not. They traveled through the desert all that night. And in the morning the man waved his hand in the air and a great fine palace appeared before them.

The man said, "We're going to that palace. When we get there, I don't want you to say a word." So he waved his hand again, and the air shifted, so that now they were standing where the palace was. Only it wasn't a palace, it was a little brick house. The man climbed on top of it, and said some words, and the wind took them, and dropped them in a lonely spot, by a great big stone. The man waved his hands, and said some words, and the stone broke wide open, revealing a metal door.

The man gave the boy a magic wand to open the door. He told him, "In there are fields of beautiful flowers. Pick as many as you can, and bring them to me. But do not say a word. If you speak, I cannot help you."

The lad went in and started picking the beautiful flowers. There were flowers of every color and every kind, and wonderful fruits too. Soon he had all the flowers and fruit that he could hold. So he brought them to the entrance, and called, "I've got them!"

As he spoke a word, wild beasts rushed at him from every side.

He waved the wand, and the metal door opened for him to get out.

The man was there, and he was furious with the boy for disobeying him. "I told you not to speak a word!"

"But I have brought you the flowers and fruit. Look!" And the lad held out his armfuls of flowers.

"Flowers and fruit! If you had not spoken, they would have been jewels and riches. You are a useless boy." With that, the man waved his hand in the air and disappeared. The boy was left all alone.

The young fellow did not know what to do, now that the man had abandoned him in the wilderness. He began to rub the magic wand, muttering, "What now?"

At that moment a funny little bearded man appeared. The lad was scared, but the bearded man said, "Don't be afraid of me. I am the friend of all who hold the magic wand. I will carry you to any place you want. I am the demon of the wand, and I will obey you."

"Take me away from this place," said the lad.

So the demon flew and flew and dropped the lad down in the desert. He was all alone by himself, with no one to speak to and nothing to eat. He was worrying and worrying, and he rubbed the wand again, muttering, "What now?"

The little bearded man appeared again. "What's the matter?" he asked.

"I am hungry," the young fellow said.

The bearded man busied himself, and in a few minutes a grand hotel had risen from the desert, full of servants who were there to serve the lad and to honor him as a king.

"Is there anything else you want?" asked the bearded man.

"New clothes," said the lad, and he got a suit as fine as a king's.

After that he stayed there, but he got tired of living like a prince, all alone in the desert. He rubbed the wand again, muttering, "What now?"

"What do you want?" asked the bearded man.

"I want you to take away all this and give me a horse. I want to go out and make my fortune. I want to make my own living."

So the bearded man did as he asked.

The young fellow rode until he came to a city, and he saw a beautiful princess there. He just stared at the princess.

A man said, "What are you looking at? If the king catches you looking at the princess, he will kill you. It's against the law."

The young fellow learned that the princess had one flaw in her beauty; she could not laugh. The king had sent for all the wise men in the world, but they could not help her. So the king decreed that whoever could make his daughter laugh should marry her.

The lad thought and thought how to make the princess laugh, and then he rubbed the wand again.

"What do you want?" asked the bearded man.

"I want to make the princess laugh," he said. "First you have to get me the finest suit that ever a prince wore, of gold, diamonds, silver, and gold buttons. I want the finest horse

that ever lived. I want footmen dressed in gold and silver. I want bags of gold, diamonds, and jewels of every kind."

So he went to the princess, riding his white horse, with his line of footmen. He had the peculiarest walking stick that ever was known, see. That walking stick could dance, sing, and squeal like a pig. The princess just had to laugh.

So the king gave his consent for them to be married. But he said, "Before you marry her, I want you to build a palace for my daughter, opposite my own."

The young fellow called up the bearded man, and asked him for the finest palace the world had ever known. He said, "I want diamonds, and silver, and shiny gold. I want doorknobs of gold, and a roof glistening with gold. It must be finer than the king's own palace."

Everyone thought it was magic. No one thought anyone could build a palace like that overnight; it should have taken seven years.

So the lad and the princess were married, see, and went to live there, see, and lived happily ever after, see.

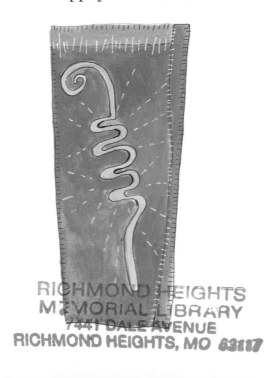

RICHMOND HEIGHTS
MEMORIAL LIBRARY
7441 DALE AVENUE
RICHMOND HEIGHTS, MO 63117

# THE LITTLE BULL WITH THE GOLDEN HORNS

## Missouri

It's good to tell you, once there was an old man and an old woman. They had a boy and they called him Little John. When he grew up, Little John became a farmer. Little John's neighbor was Big Devil. Big Devil wanted to be a farmer too, but he didn't know how, and besides he didn't have a team.

One day he went to ask Little John to help him sow some wheat. "All right," said Little John, "that's fine. We'll sow a crop of wheat." Next spring when the wheat was ripe, Big Devil went to ask Little John if it was ready to cut, as he didn't know the first thing about farming. When Little John thought it was ready, he went to see, and it was. So he said, "We'll start cutting our wheat tomorrow, Big Devil. It's ripe."

They went into the field. Big Devil wanted to know how they were going to separate the wheat. "Well," said Little John, "we've got to cut it, then we've got to thresh it, and then we separate it."

"No," said Big Devil, "I want to separate it right away."

"Fine, if you want to separate it right away, go ahead. But how do you aim to do it?"

"I'll tell you what we'll do," said Big Devil. "I'll take the roots."

"All right," said Little John. "You take the roots, and I'll take the tops." So Little John got all the grain and all the straw, while Big Devil was left with the roots.

Big Devil went to find Little John while he was threshing the wheat. "You stole all the wheat, Little John," he said.

"Hmm," said Little John. "It was you who separated it."

"Yes," he said, "but you knew better, Little John. You should have told me right away. You stole it all."

In the fall he went to find Little John again, to plant some turnips. "All right," said Little John. "That's fine. We'll plant turnips." So they planted a great turnip patch.

When they were ready to lift, Big Devil said, "Well, we must divide our turnips."

"All right," said Little John. "But last time you said I stole all the wheat, so it's your turn to separate the turnips."

"Yes, and I won't let you trick me again, Little John," said Big Devil. "I'll take the tops this time."

"All right," said Little John. "You take the tops, and I'll take the roots."

Big Devil went and cut all the tops off the turnip plants and took them. Little John went behind him, pulling up the turnips, and took them. Big Devil took all the leaves and stems to his house and tried to cook and eat them, but it was hopeless.

And all this while, Little John had all the turnips. "Little John," said Big Devil, "you cheated me again. You stole all the turnips."

"I stole them? It was you who separated them; you took everything you wanted."

"Yes," said Big Devil, "but you knew better."

"So, Big Devil," he said, "you're calling me a thief, huh? Well, mark my words, now I *will* rob you."

"Little John, you'd better not try any such thing, or I'll gobble you up like a grain of salt."

Nothing happened for a while, but then Little John got bored of being alone. He went to see the king and asked if he could move in with him. "Oh, yes," said the king, "I'd love you to move in with me. I'd like the company." The king had a fine house, and Little John was as happy as could be. But after a while he grew sad and spent all his time deep in thought. The king asked what was on his mind.

"Big Devil has a little fiddle," he said. "I'm thinking what a good time we would have if only we had that fiddle. We could have a party. Wouldn't that be fun!"

"Yes, Little John," said the king. "But it's not possible. Leave it alone, or you'll get yourself killed."

"Oh!" said Little John. "I won't try to do it. I only said, if we had it, we could have a good time."

One day, he said to the king, "I fancy going out visiting tonight."

"Fine," said the king. "Go and visit the neighbors."

So Little John went out visiting. First he had to cross a big river. When he got to the other side, he went to Big Devil's house. He listened outside, and he could hear Big Devil playing his fiddle. "Come on," Little John said. "It's time for bed." He went right up to the fence and hid behind a post. Big Devil played his fiddle right up to the time he fell asleep; then the fiddle slid from his hands onto the porch. Little John waited till he was sound asleep, and then tiptoed up and took the little fiddle and the bow and ran off.

Soon Big Devil woke and looked all around him for his fiddle, but he couldn't find it anywhere. "Well," he said. "Little John must have stolen my fiddle." He ran to the river, but he was too late, he couldn't catch him.

Little John got back to the king's house. He was so pleased

with himself, he played the fiddle all night long. That livened up the house! But after a while Little John grew bored and fell to thinking again. The king said, "What's on your mind, Little John?"

"Big Devil has a sun," he said. "If we had that sun, we wouldn't need a lamp. That would be good."

"Leave it alone," said the king. "You can't steal it. You'll get yourself killed."

"All right, king," he said. "I didn't say I was going to steal it."

A couple of nights later Little John said he was going out visiting. "Fine," said the king. "Go out if you want, but listen to me: don't go and steal Big Devil's sun. You'll get yourself killed."

So Little John went out visiting. He went up to Big Devil's fence and hid behind a post.

That day was Big Devil's wife's washday. She had all her linen hung up to dry outside. "Now," said Little John, "if only she would take the sun outside while she takes in her washing, I could steal it."

"Oh!" said the old woman. "I've forgotten to bring the washing in, and now it's getting dark."

The old man said, "Hang the sun on the end of the porch, and then you can see to bring it in."

So she hung the sun on the end of the porch and took in all her washing. She had too big an armful of washing to carry the sun too, so she left it hanging outside. When she went inside with her washing, Little John took the sun.

After Big Devil's wife had put her linen away, she said, "I'd better go and fetch the sun in." But when she went to get it, it was gone. She could just see it glimmering, away in the distance. "Oh!" she said. "Someone has stolen the sun."

The old man got up and said, "This is one of Little John's tricks."

He began to run as fast as he could after him. When he arrived at the riverbank, he shouted, "Hey! Little John! You stole my sun! I'll get you, you'll see!"

When Little John got back, he hung the sun up in the house and woke up the king. "Come and see how it brightens up the house," he said. "It's just great to have a house as light as this."

The king and the queen got up and spent the rest of the night admiring the sun. The king said, "Yes, it's really lovely. But you shouldn't have done it, Little John. You'll get yourself killed."

So for a while Little John was quite content in the king's house. How beautiful it was!

But after some months Little John fell into a gloom again. He was thinking hard. The king said, "Little John, what's on your mind?"

"Well," he said, "I'm thinking that Big Devil has a little bull with golden horns, and that if we had that, we wouldn't want for anything."

"Yes," said the king, "that would be nice, Little John. But I'm telling you, leave it alone. You'll get yourself killed."

"Oh!" said Little John. "There's no danger of that."

One evening he said, "I fancy visiting the neighbors."

"You can go to the neighbors, but don't go stealing the little bull with the golden horns. You'll get yourself killed."

"Oh, no!" he said. "I won't go anywhere near it."

He crossed the river. The little bull with the golden horns was sleeping right by the fence. He waited for Big Devil to fall asleep while he thought what to do.

As soon as Little John caught hold of the little bull with the golden horns, it began to bellow. *Weuh! Weuh! Weuh!* That woke up Big Devil, who ran after Little John. But Little John had crossed the river before he could catch him. Big Devil shouted, "Hey! Little John! You've stolen everything I had in the world!"

"Yes," said Little John. "I've stolen everything you had. And I'm going to steal you too."

"If you come anywhere near me, Little John, I'll gobble you up like a grain of salt."

Little John took the little bull back to the king's house and put him in a corner. He woke up the king to see the little bull with the golden horns. Oh! How happy he was!

Little John fetched the sun to light up the little bull. The king said it was the best little bull he had ever seen. Then Little John fetched the fiddle and played it all night long. So for a while Little John was quite content. But then one day he fell to brooding again. He fretted and grew listless.

The king noticed and suggested he should get out of the house and find something to do. There was a blacksmith's forge nearby; he could spend the day there.

So Little John went over to the forge to spend the day. He said to the smith, "Could you make an iron coach?"

"Oh, yes," he said. "I could make one."

Little John said, "I want one so strong it would take eight horses to pull it."

"I'll make it for you," said the the smith.

Every day Little John went to the forge to see how the iron coach was coming along. When it was finished, he went to the king and asked for eight of the best horses he had. "What do you want them for, Little John?" the king asked.

"What difference does it make what I want them for? I want eight of your best horses."

"Little John, I won't lend you my horses unless you tell me what you want them for."

"Fine. If you don't want to lend me the horses, you can keep them."

"Little John," said the king, "I can't refuse you anything. If you want to get yourself killed, go ahead and take them."

Little John took eight of the king's best horses to the forge and hitched them to the iron coach. Then he disguised himself in old clothes, an old cap, and a false beard. He looked completely different. Then he drove the iron coach by Big Devil's house. He had left the door open so that it would bang shut at every bump and make a noise. When he went by Big Devil's house, he shouted at the horses, "Whoop! Whoop!" The door banged to, *Vring! Vrang!*

Big Devil came out to see what was making all the row. He couldn't imagine what in the world it could be. He shouted, "Hey! Hey! Come back!"

"Whoa!" Little John pulled up and went back to Big Devil.

"What on earth are you doing with that?" asked Big Devil. He didn't recognize who it was. He said, "I want to catch Little John. He stole everything I had in the world, so I want to take him and stuff him in that coach and lock the door."

"Tell me about it," said Little John. "He stole everything I had too. So I'm going to tell you just where he is."

"Where is he?"

"He is on the other side of the river, in the king's house."

"Do you think that iron coach would hold him?" asked Big Devil.

"Yes, I think it would."

"That's what worries me," said Big Devil. "His power is

so great, I'm afraid it wouldn't be strong enough to hold him."

Little John said, "You must be as strong as he is. Why don't you get in the coach and see if it would hold him?"

"Oh, yes, I think it would," said Big Devil.

"Let's make sure," said Little John. "Get inside, and we will try it out."

So Big Devil got in the iron coach, and Little John slammed the door shut. After he had locked the door, he said, "Try to get out! You must be as strong as he is."

Big Devil tried to open the door, but he couldn't. "Yes, it will hold him," he said.

"You didn't push hard enough! Try again," said Little John.

While Big Devil struggled to get out of the iron coach, Little John took off his beard, his old cap, his old clothes, everything, and put on his own clothes again. Then he went to where Big Devil could see him.

"Ah! Little John!" said Big Devil. "Is that you?"

"Yes," he said. "It's me. You called me a thief, and I said I would steal you, and I have."

"Hey! Hey!" said Big Devil. "Let me out of here, Little John!"

But Little John said, "I'm taking you to the king."

He drove the coach to the king's house. When he got there, he unhitched the horses and put them in the stable. Then he went back to the iron coach and shouted for the king to come and see what he had in there.

The king came out to see. He was carrying an iron pitch-fork. When he got to the coach, he banged on the side with the

pitchfork. There was a great roar from inside, and the king ran away.

"Come back, you sissy," said Little John. "There's nothing to be afraid of."

So the king came back and banged on the side of the coach with the iron pitchfork a second time. "Roar! Roar!" went Big Devil, and the king got scared again and ran away.

"Come back, you sissy," said Little John. "There's no need to be afraid. He can't get out."

So the king came back and looked in the iron coach and saw Big Devil in there.

Big Devil pleaded, "Oh, Little John, if you let me go, I'll give you my word in writing that you'll never see me again."

"You can cry all you want, Big Devil. I've got you where I want you, and I'll keep you there to the end of your days!"

But after a while, Little John got bored with that too, and he let Big Devil go home.

# THE GOLD IN THE CHIMNEY

## Kentucky

Once upon a time there were two girls. They were sisters, and one went to a witch's house to get a place to stay. Well, the witch said, "All right, you can stay." Then she said, "I'm going to the store. Don't look up the chimney while I'm gone."

While the witch was gone, the girl looked up the chimney. There hung a bag of gold. She took it and set off.

She came to a cow. The cow said, "Please milk me, little girl. I ain't been milked in several long years."

She said, "I ain't got time."

She went on and came to a sheep. The sheep said, "Please shear me, little girl. I ain't been sheared in several long years."

She said, "I ain't got time."

She went on and came to a horse. The horse said, "Please ride me, little girl, I ain't been rode in several long years."

She said, "I ain't got time."

She went on and came to a mill. The mill said, "Please turn me, little girl, I ain't been turned in several long years."

The little girl said, "I ain't got time." She went over and lay down behind the door and went to sleep.

Well, the old witch came back, and her gold was gone. She started out and came to the cow, and said:

73

> Cow o' mine, cow o' mine,
> Have you seen a maid o' mine,
> With a wig and a wag and a long leather bag,
> Who stole all the money I ever had?

The cow said, "Yeah, she just passed."
She went on to the sheep, and said:

> Sheep o' mine, sheep o' mine,
> Have you seen a maid o' mine,
> With a wig and a wag and a long leather bag,
> Who stole all the money I ever had?

The sheep said, "Yeah, she just passed."
She went on to the horse, and said,

> Horse o' mine, horse o' mine,
> Have you seen a maid o' mine,
> With a wig and a wag and a long leather bag,
> Who stole all the money I ever had?

The horse said, "Yeah, she just passed."
She went on to the mill, and said:

> Mill o' mine, mill o' mine,
> Have you seen a maid o' mine,
> With a wig and a wag and a long leather bag,
> Who stole all the money I ever had?

It said, "She's layin' over there behind the door."
The witch went over and turned her into a stone. She got her gold and went on back home.

Well, the second girl came along and said, "Can I stay here?"

The witch said, "Yeah, but I'm going to the store." Then she said, "Don't look up the chimney while I'm gone."

When the witch was gone, the girl looked up the chimney.

There hung this bag of gold. She took it and set out for home.

She came to the cow, and the cow said, "Please milk me, little girl. I ain't been milked in several long years."

She milked the cow.

She went on to the sheep. The sheep said, "Please shear me, little girl. I ain't been sheared in several long years."

She sheared the sheep.

She went on to the horse. The horse said, "Please ride me, little girl. I ain't been rode in several long years."

So she rode the horse.

Then she came to the mill. The mill said, "Please turn me, little girl. I ain't been turned in several long years."

She turned the mill.

Then she lay down behind the door and went to sleep.

Well, the old witch got back, and her gold was gone. She started out. She came to the cow, and said:

> Cow o' mine, cow o' mine,
> Have you seen a maid o' mine,
> With a wig and a wag and a long leather bag,
> Who stole all the money I ever had?

The cow said, "No."

She went to the sheep, and said:

> Sheep o' mine, sheep o' mine,
> Have you seen a maid o' mine,
> With a wig and a wag and a long leather bag,
> Who stole all the money I ever had?

The sheep said, "No, I ain't never seen her."

She went on to the horse, and said:

> Horse o' mine, horse o' mine,
> Have you seen a maid o' mine,

> With a wig and a wag and a long leather bag,
> Who stole all the money I ever had?

The horse said, "No, I ain't never seen her."
She went on to the mill, and said:

> Mill o' mine, mill o' mine,
> Have you seen a maid o' mine,
> With a wig and a wag and a long leather bag,
> Who stole all the money I ever had?

It said, "Get in my hopper, I can't hear good."
She got up in the hopper, and shouted:

> MILL O' MINE, MILL O' MINE,
> HAVE YOU SEEN A MAID O' MINE,
> WITH A WIG AND A WAG AND A LONG
>   LEATHER BAG,
> WHO STOLE ALL THE MONEY I EVER HAD?

And the mill started grinding, and ground her up.
The little girl got up from behind the door, turned the stone
back into her sister, and they lived happy ever after.

# THREE EILESCHPIJJEL STORIES

**Pennsylvania**

## In the Windy Poconos

Eileschpijjel was servant to a farmer up in the Poconos. One day he was sent out into a field with a two-horse team to pick stones and haul them to a stone fence.

Eileschpijjel drove into the field, which was literally covered with stones. When he saw the endlessness of his task, he quit and drove home.

"What's wrong?" asked the farmer.

"It is so windy out in the field that whenever I throw stones on the wagon from one side, the wind blows them down on the other side. Such work I do not like, and I am leaving for another job until the stones have been plowed under and the field is fit to work in," said Eileschpijjel.

## The Wagon Load

Eileschpijjel went with a two-horse team for wood. As he threw each piece on the wagon, he said, "If the horses can pull this piece, they can pull the next one."

Reasoning thus, he kept on loading until the wagon was completely filled. Then he found that the horses were unable to pull the load.

He proceeded to unload the wagon, saying as he threw off each piece, "If they can't pull this piece, they can't pull the next one."

Reasoning thus, he kept on unloading until the wagon was empty.

Then he drove home with an empty wagon.

# Eileschpijjel the Plowman

Eileschpijjel was hired by a farmer to plow. The farmer went with him into the field where he was to plow.

"How shall I plow?" asked Eileschpijjel.

There was a hog at the other end of the field, and the farmer, pointing to it, said, "Plow all the way to the hog and back."

In the evening, when Eileschpijjel brought the horses into the barn, the farmer asked, "Is there still much to be plowed?"

"It all depends on how far the hog will go," answered Eileschpijjel.

# JACK AND THE BEANSTALK

## Kentucky

Once upon a time there was a mother and her son, Jack, living in wealth. One night a great giant came to their house and took from them a bag of gold, their magic harp, and their little hen that laid golden eggs. They never had a thing left but an old brown cow.

One morning his mother sent Jack to market to trade the old brown cow for some grub. About dusty dark that evening Jack came back home. His mother was uneasy about Jack because there was no food in the house and she was hungry. When she saw Jack coming, she ran out to the paling fence to meet him.

"Well, Jack, what did you get in trade for the old brown cow?"

Jack said:

> I traded my cow for a little red calf,
> And in that trade I just lost half;
> I traded my calf for a little pink pig,
> It wa'n't worth much 'cause it wa'n't very big;
> I traded my pig for a little white mouse,
> He wouldn't say please and he wouldn't keep house;
> So I traded my mouse for a little white bean,
> The purtiest bean you ever have seen.

Jack's mother flew so mad she threw the little white bean out of the window into the yard.

Next morning when Jack looked out of the window, he saw a great big beanstalk growing in the yard, stretching up and up into the sky as far as he could see. Jack began to climb up the beanstalk while his mother was gone to the woods to see if she could find something for them to eat. He climbed and climbed and climbed until he came to the top of the beanstalk.

He saw such a tall building, he decided it must be a giant's land up there. Jack went up to the giant's house and knocked on the door, pretending to be a newsboy selling papers. The door came open, and an old woman looked out at him.

Jack said, "Good morning, old woman. My name is Jack."

The old woman said, "Jack, you are a brave boy to come here." She listened out. Then she whispered softly, "Jack, hide in this kettle right now! I hear the giant coming."

In came the old giant, saying:

> Fee, fie, foe, fum,
> One, two, three, and here I come;
> Fum, foe, fie, fee,
> Here I come, one, two, three;
> Bring my little hen
> That lays the golden eggs.

The old woman brought the little hen, and it began to sing:

> Cack, cack-a-dack.
> Cack, cack-a-dack.

While the hen sang, the giant went to sleep.

Jack slipped out of the kettle and grabbed the little hen, and

away he ran. The little hen knew Jack, and she began to sing for him. This waked up the old giant, and he took off down the road after Jack. But Jack climbed down the beanstalk and ran home.

He ran in the door and said, "Look, Mommy, I brought back the little hen that the giant stole from us." The hen began to sing for Jack's mother.

While the mother was talking to the little hen, Jack climbed back up the beanstalk. When the old woman saw him at the door again, she said, "Jack, the giant is mad, and hunting all over the place for you. I hear him coming now. Here, hide in the kettle quick!"

Jack just got in the kettle when he heard the giant:

> Fee, fie, foe, fum,
> One, two, three, and here I come;
> Fum, foe, fie, fee,
> Here I come, one, two, three;
> Bring me my magic harp.

The old woman brought the harp, and it began to sing:

> Harper, harper, where are you?
> Come and play a tune or two.
> In the summer or in the spring
> Play the strings and I will sing.

As the harp sang and played, the giant fell asleep.

Jack eased out of the kettle and grabbed the harp, and away he went. The harp was so happy it began to sing louder. This woke the giant up, and he began to chase Jack.

Jack climbed down the beanstalk and ran to his mother and said, "Look, Mommy, I brought back the golden harp the giant stole from us." The harp and the little hen were so glad to be home, they both sang together.

Jack decided to climb the beanstalk again. He climbed right up to the giant's land. He knocked on the door, and before the old woman could run him off, she heard the giant coming. Jack ran and jumped in the kettle.

The giant came in.

> Fee, fie, foe, fum,
> One, two, three, and here I come:
> Fum, foe, fie, fee,
> Here I come, one, two, three;
> Bring me my money bag.

85

The old woman brought him his moneybag. The giant said:

> Money, money, sing to me.

The money sang out:

> Diamonds, rubies, emeralds too,
> Sparkling like the dew.
> Count them over one by one,
> Sparkling like the sun.

This made the giant go to sleep. As soon as Jack heard him snoring he jumped out of the kettle, grabbed the moneybag off the table, and took off. The moneybag began to sing louder, and this woke the old giant. He was so mad at Jack, he meant to kill him and eat him this time. He was going to follow Jack home.

Jack hit the beanstalk and climbed down faster than ever before, but the giant was gaining on him. When he got down near the earth, Jack dropped the moneybag so he could climb faster. Before he reached the ground, his mother saw the giant after Jack, so she ran and got an ax, and Jack cut the beanstalk down.

It fell with a big crash. The giant hit the ground so hard he bounced back up into giant-land.

# THE BIG CABBAGE

## Michigan

One fellow said, "You know, my grandfather was the best farmer in Florida. He raised a cabbage so large a regiment of soldiers could stand under one leaf."

Other fellow said, "Well, my grandfather made him a pot so large it took a train running ninety miles an hour six weeks to go around it."

Other fellow says, "What do you want with a pot like that?"

"Well, to cook that lying cabbage your granddaddy raised."

# TOBE KILLED A BEAR

## Missouri

One time there was a fellow named Tobe that lived up on the Cowskin, and he was the stoutest man ever come to this country. He was near seven foot tall and weighed three hundred pounds.

Tobe was a good worker and a terrible fighter, but not very smart. He would do whatever you told him, so long as he didn't get mad, and then he was liable to do most anything. One Sunday he threw a fiddler pretty near halfway across the river. The fiddler would have drowned for sure, only some of the boys swum out and got him.

The country was full of bears in them days, and a great big bear got to hanging around the Widow Tarkey's smokehouse. It would bust in the door and gobble up everything in sight.

The widow lived by herself, and she was scared pretty bad, so she asked Tobe to come over and kill the varmint. He come over, all right, but he didn't bring no gun. "The bear ain't got no gun, has he?" says Tobe. "That makes us even, and I aim to fight him fair."

Tobe was one of them fellows that goes to sleep whenever he sets down, and that's what happened on the widow's porch. But when the bear busted the smokehouse door, it woke him up, and he ran out there. Tobe and the bear fought something terrible, and the Widow Tarkey figured Tobe

would get killed for sure. But after a while he came back up the path.

"Did you kill the critter?" says the widow.

"I reckon not, ma'am," says Tobe, "but he won't bother your smokehouse no more," and with that he threw about fifty pounds of bear meat down on the porch. Tobe had torn one of that bear's legs right off, just pulled it out by the roots!

Next day the boys followed the trail down the riverbank, and they found the bear in a cave, but he was dead. One of his front legs was gone, all right, torn off right at the shoulder. The varmint had spilled a barrel of blood, and that's what killed him.

Mostly the folks figured it was a lie, because everybody knows there ain't no man stout enough to pull the leg off a bear like it was a June bug. They saw the leg all right, nailed up over the smokehouse door, with claws a-sticking out four inches long. "That don't prove nothing," says Wes Galbraith. "They got elk horns nailed on the tavern at Pea Ridge, but nobody claims they tore 'em off a live elk barehanded."

There was considerable talk about it. Tobe says this is a free country, and folks can believe whatever they want. But if anybody calls him a liar, he will pull their arms and legs off one at a time, right in front of the courthouse. Wes Galbraith and them Rutledge boys didn't have no more to say after that.

Nobody ever did find out just what happened, and Tobe's been dead for fifty years. But there's old settlers around here yet that believe Tobe did pull the bear's leg off, just like he told the Widow Tarkey.

# THE CAT THAT WENT A-TRAVELING

**Kentucky**

This here olden tale says a cat heard an old woman say she was going to kill it, for no good reason but she hated cats. The old cat gathered up her kittens and set out a-traveling.

Down the road a piece she met up with a dog. She told the dog how come she was a-traveling. The dog said, "Think I'll

91

just go along with you. Folks don't treat me too good where I been living. Won't let me lay by the fire in the wintertime."

The cat said, "Come along and welcome."

A little piece on down the road, they met up with a cow. They told the cow how come they were a-traveling. The cow said, "Think I'll just go along with you. Folks don't treat me too good where I been living. Don't feed me nothing but little, old nubbins."

They said, "Come along and welcome."

Next they met up with a guinea hen. They told the guinea hen how come they were a-traveling. The guinea hen said, "Think I'll just go along with you. Folks don't treat me too good where I been living. They hunt my nest in the high weeds and take out my eggs with a big spoon."

They said, "Come along and welcome."

After that they met a gander. They told the gander how come they were a-traveling. The gander said, "Think I'll just go along with you. Folks don't treat me too good where I been

living. Pick all my feathers off of my back and sides to make them a featherbed."

They said, "Come along and welcome."

Then they met a rooster. They told the rooster how come they were a-traveling. The rooster said, "Think I'll just go along with you. Folks where I live don't treat me too good. Been talking about killing me to make a big pot of chicken and dumplings."

They said, "Come along and welcome."

They kept on a-traveling till nigh-dark. Then they found a little house. Seemed like nobody was living there. So they took up for the night. The dog lay by the fire. The rooster and the guinea hen flew up to the rafters. The cow stood behind the door. The gander squatted in a corner. And the cat and her kittens took the bed for their share.

In the night all the animal creatures woke up with the voice of some men talking in the little house. They listened, and it was robbers counting the money they stole. The animal creatures were scared so bad they made their own noises as loud as they could. The cat and her kittens mewed, the dog barked, the cow mooed, the guinea hen pot-racked, the rooster crowed, and the gander screamed and hissed.

All the animal creatures named in this here tale are mighty noisy creatures, and all put together they scared the robbers so bad they ran off and left their money.

The cat said, "They'll be back. They won't give up the money they stole without trying." So the animal creatures planned out how they would scare the robbers so bad they would stay gone after that.

The next night the robbers came sneaking back to get their

money. All at the same time and in the dark, the animals made their noises, and acted out what they planned. The cat and her kittens mewed and scratched. The dog barked and bit. The cow mooed and kicked. The guinea hen pot-racked and pecked at the robbers' eyes. The rooster done the same thing and crowed. The gander screamed and hissed and beat the robbers with his wings.

Hearing all the different noises mixed together at the same time, the robbers had no idea what all it might be. And being come at in the dark with all them things trying to hurt them made the robbers scared of their lives. They ran off in the dark and left their money again and never did come back.

The cat took the little house for her home and let all the animal creatures live with her and her kittens. They used the money the robbers left to live on, for they had no idea who it belonged to and couldn't give it back. The robbers ought not had it, for they never came by it honest.

# THE ENCHANTED PRINCE

## New Mexico

Once there was a woman who had nine daughters. The oldest had nine eyes, the next had eight eyes, the next seven eyes, the next six eyes, the next five, the next four, the next three, the next one eye, and the youngest two eyes.

One day the daughters went out for a walk through a forest, and the youngest one, the one who had two eyes, left the others and met a beautiful green bird, and he asked her to marry him. He told her that he was an enchanted prince and that if she did as he asked, she would someday be a queen. Two Eyes promised to marry him and agreed to do what he asked. Green Bird then flew away.

Two Eyes went to her sisters and told them all about her meeting with the bird. They immediately began to make fun of her. "What are you going to do with a bird?" they asked her. "He will take you away to a nest somewhere."

"It is my wish," she replied. "I am going to marry him even if he is a bird." And from there they went home to tell their mother.

Soon the bird arrived to ask for Two Eyes in marriage. The mother and sisters objected. But Two Eyes insisted and finally went away with the bird and married him. Green Bird took her to the mountains, to a beautiful palace. He gave his bride the keys to all the rooms of the palace. He told her again that he was an enchanted prince, to be very careful, and not to say a word about the enchantment.

He also told her that the palace had nine windows, and that he would be with her only during the night; he would fly away in the morning and come to sing at each of the nine windows at nine o'clock, and then stay for the night. He then gave her a little bottle of sleeping water and told her to put some on the sheets of the bed so that anyone sleeping on it would go to sleep and would not see him or hear him sing. The bird then flew away for the first time.

The mother of the daughters was envious. She called Nine Eyes and said to her, "You must go now to see your sister in order to find out who the bird is. You have nine eyes and can see more than your sisters." Nine Eyes left at once.

When Nine Eyes arrived at her sister's beautiful palace, Two Eyes went out to meet her, took her inside, and showed her the nine windows of the palace. "But I don't see your husband, Green Bird, anywhere," she said. Two Eyes did not say anything in reply.

Finally Nine Eyes got tired of seeing all the things the palace contained and said she wished to go to bed. Two Eyes took her to a bed and secretly put a few drops of the sleeping water on the sheets. Nine Eyes went to sleep immediately.

Green Bird arrived at nine o'clock as he had promised and sang beautifully at each of the nine windows of the palace, but Nine Eyes didn't see anything or hear anything. Then he entered the palace as a handsome prince. He asked his wife, "Who came here?"

"My sister, Nine Eyes," replied Two Eyes.

"Well and good," said the prince. "If there is no envy,

everything is all right; but if there is envy, and we get into trouble, I will leave and you will never see me again."

Before dawn he left again, having told his wife to give her sister anything she wished from the things she had in the palace.

In the morning Nine Eyes woke up and went to see her sister. She was surprised that she had seen nothing of the bird. She asked Two Eyes, but Two Eyes said nothing that would satisfy her curiosity; she remembered what her husband had told her and did not wish to betray him. Nine Eyes then went

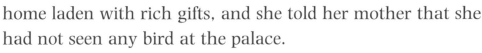

home laden with rich gifts, and she told her mother that she had not seen any bird at the palace.

The next night Eight Eyes was sent to the palace. "Your sister who has nine eyes has not seen the bird," said the mother. "Now let us see whether you can see anything."

She arrived at the palace and asked about the bird, but Two Eyes merely took her around and showed her the palace, the nine windows, and everything else. She fell asleep immediately after Two Eyes put her to bed with sleeping water on the sheets. At nine o'clock Green Bird appeared again, sang at the nine windows, and again stayed the night with his wife. Eight Eyes did not see or hear anything.

The same thing happened to Seven Eyes, to Six Eyes, to Five Eyes, to Four Eyes, and to Three Eyes. All did as Nine Eyes and Eight Eyes had done. Each of them went to sleep and saw nothing. And each evening, while they were in the palace asleep, Green Bird arrived at nine o'clock, sang at each one of the nine windows, and remained all night with his wife without being seen by any of them.

"Now we must be more careful than ever," the prince said to his wife. "If there is no envy, I shall soon be disenchanted, and we will be king and queen."

One Eye said to her mother and her sisters, "I have only one eye, but I am going to show you that I can see more than all of you together."

The next morning, after Green Bird had flown away to the mountains, Two Eyes looked out of one of her windows and saw One Eye coming. "Well, there is my one-eyed sister coming to see me," she said. She awaited her gladly and, as soon as she arrived, went out to meet her.

"How are you, my sister?" asked One Eye.

"Very well indeed," said Two Eyes. "You must let me show you the palace that Green Bird, my husband, gave me."

"I am too tired," said One Eye. "I really don't care to see anything. Now that I have seen you, I think I had better go home."

"Oh, no," said Two Eyes, "you must stay for dinner!"

Finally she stayed. At night she went to bed, but Two Eyes did not put sleeping water on the sheets. "My sister One Eye is so small and so tired, she will not see anything," she said to herself.

When One Eye went to bed, she said to Two Eyes, "Cover me up with the sheet." But when Two Eyes went away, she made a hole in the sheet to look through.

At nine o'clock Green Bird arrived and sang at the nine windows, and One Eye saw and heard everything. She was covered with the sheet, but she could see through the hole with her one eye. When the bird sang at the last window, he became a handsome prince, as he did every evening, and One Eye saw everything.

"Good evening, my love," said the prince to Two Eyes. "Who came this evening?"

"My sister, my little sister," replied Two Eyes.

"Yes, I know all about it," said the prince. "You have been ungrateful and unfaithful to me. Tomorrow you will see me leave in a carriage drawn by a black crow." Then he went away, leaving Two Eyes very sad.

"What did you see, sister?" asked Two Eyes of One Eye late in the morning when she got up.

"Nothing, I didn't see anything. Please give me my breakfast so that I can go home." Two Eyes gave her her breakfast, and she left. Then Two Eyes remained alone, abandoned by her sisters and by her husband.

As soon as One Eye reached home, she told her mother and her sisters all she had seen. "My sisters with so many eyes could not see anything, and I with just one eye have seen everything," she said.

When the envious mother had heard everything, she said, "This evening I am going myself." And she did as she said. She went secretly and placed pieces of sharp glass in all the windows, so that the bird would cut himself and die, and she and her daughters would come to possess the beautiful palace. As soon as she had done the mischief, she left.

The bird arrived at nine, as was his custom, and began to sing at the first window. He sang well there, but as he continued to sing at the other windows, his voice became weaker and weaker, because he was all cut up with the broken glass the mother of Two Eyes had placed in the windows. He entered his room very weak and said to Two Eyes, "What an ungrateful thing you have done! Now I must leave, as I told you. You will never see me again." A carriage appeared, drawn by a black crow; the wounded prince entered it and soon disappeared from view.

Two Eyes almost died of grief. But she watched the direction the carriage had taken, and taking her royal garments and her little bottle of sleeping water with her, she departed in search of her husband. She traveled and traveled, and finally, almost exhausted, she sat down at the foot of a poplar to rest.

Presently she heard some birds in the tree conversing. One

bird was saying that the prince was very ill, and that there was only one way he could be cured. "How can he be cured?" asked another bird.

"By someone killing us and taking the blood and anointing the wounds of the prince with it. In that way all the glass will come out, and he will get well."

When Two Eyes heard this, she emptied the sleeping water out of her little bottle over the roots of the tree. The little birds then went to sleep, and she killed them all and put their blood in the bottle. Then she went her way in search of the prince, her husband. She searched and searched but could not find him.

Finally she went to see the moon. She asked the moon whether she had seen a sick prince anywhere. "I have been at the window of every house in the world and have not seen such a prince," said the moon.

Then she went to see the sun. She asked the sun the same question. "Indeed I have seen him," replied the sun. "He is very ill at his father's house. I cannot take you there, but maybe the wind can take you."

Two Eyes then went to see the wind. "Yes indeed, I know that prince well," said the wind. "The king, his father, has brought doctors from all parts of the world, but none can cure him. If you wish, I can take you to where he is."

Two Eyes thanked him and asked him to take her at once. "Get inside this leather bag and take this knife with you," said the wind. "I will blow you there, and as you land, cut a hole in the bag with the knife and climb out."

A great wind arose and blew the bag to the house of the king. When it was grounded, Two Eyes cut a hole through the leather and got out. She went to the door of the palace and asked the servants about the prince. "He is very ill," they said. "The doctors say he will surely die."

Then she told them to tell the king that if they would allow her to go into the palace, she could cure the prince. The king said that she could come in. When she entered, the king told her, "If you can really cure the prince, I will support you for the rest of your life."

She asked for a sheet and put on it the blood of the birds that she had in the little bottle. Then she ordered that the prince should be wrapped in it so the blood would cover his wounds. This she did three times, and the pieces of glass began to work their way out of the wounds. Soon all the pieces came out, and the prince was completely cured. The king then built a house for Two Eyes and said he would fulfill his promise.

The prince, however, had forgotten his former bride, and now planned to marry a beautiful princess. And Two Eyes knew everything and saw everything.

She had with her her dresses, her rings, and other presents that the prince had given her. When the day of the wedding arrived, the princess came to the king's palace to be married, because the prince was much richer than she was. And when the ceremony was about to begin, Two Eyes dressed herself in her favorite dress. When the prince entered the church with his bride-to-be, Two Eyes suddenly appeared at his side also.

The prince at once recognized her. "This is my true wife!" he said. And he left the princess and married Two Eyes.

As for the envious mother and sisters, they went to take possession of Green Bird's palace, but when they got there they found no palace at all. All they found was a deserted plain.

# MISS LIZA AND THE KING

## Georgia

Well, one time there was a king, and he was a mighty man, though what country he was a-kinging it at, and what kind of folks they were, I don't know.

He fought here, and he fought there, and by and by he grew tired of killing folks and took the idea that he had better settle down and see if he could do some good in the world.

So the king asked one of the old men if he knew of a better job than fighting. The old man combed his long gray beard with his fingernails and said, "Have you ever thought of learning a trade?"

"What do you mean?" asked the king.

"According to my notion," said the old man, "a man, king or no king, can do more good by making a pair of shoes than he can by killing a man."

This made the king bite his thumb. The old man was one of the smartest men in the kingdom, and whenever there was a problem, everyone listened to what he had to say. So the king just stood there and bit his thumb.

After a while the king asked, "How long would it take a man to learn the shoemaking trade?"

"A bright man might learn it in six or seven months," said the old man, "so I expect it will take you about a year."

"Where can I learn it?" asked the king.

"I will take you into my own shop," said the old man, "and teach you all the ins and outs of the business."

Still the king bit his thumb. "How am I going to do the kinging whilst I'm making shoes?" he asked.

"That's nothing," said the old man. "It's a heap harder to make a good pair of shoes than it is to be king, and it's a mighty slack-wadded man that can't do the kinging and learn to make shoes at the same time."

So the king said, "I'll learn to make a good pair of shoes if I have to kill every cow in the kingdom!"

Next morning the king rose bright and early, and after breakfast he told his ministers that he was going out for the day and wouldn't be back until night. Then he went to an outhouse and changed into a rough suit of clothes and set out for the shop where the old man and his men made shoes.

When the king got there, they were all pegging away as hard as they could. A young woman met him at the door and said, "Are you the new man?"

"I am," said the king.

"Well, you'll have to look sharp," she said. "My daddy

won't have no fiddling around and hanging back. There's your bench in the corner, where nobody will bother you and you won't bother anybody."

The king said, "I'm sure I would learn twice as quick if I had you to show me."

Well, she took offense at that and flounced out, ripe mad.

After a while her daddy came in, looking solemn. "One of you men has been sassing Miss Liza," he said, "and it's got to stop. She is my only daughter, and the next time one of you sasses her, I'm going to go and tell the king. He's a good friend of mine, and he'll know how to deal with you."

The new man, who was the king in disguise, said, "If it was me, I wouldn't go to the king. I'd send him a message telling him to come and see me."

Miss Lisa, listening at the door, thought that the new man couldn't be scared of anything if he wasn't scared of the king. So after a while she made out she had some business in the shop and went back in. Just one look told her that the new man didn't know any more about making shoes than the man in the moon. She said, "Who taught you how to make shoes?"

He said, "Your daddy says he is going to teach me how, but you see how it is—he thinks more of the king than he does of me."

Miss Liza said, "It's a good thing the king can't hear you, putting yourself up on the same platform as him."

"Maybe that's so," said the new man, "but every word you hear me say about the king, I would say to his face. And if he didn't like it, I would pull his whiskers; I've done it before now." And he gave his own whiskers a tug.

Miss Liza gasped. She stood there looking at the new man. "Do you mean to stand there flatfooted and tell me you pulled the king's whiskers?"

"That's what I said, and if you don't believe me, fetch the king here, where I can get my hands on him."

Miss Liza caught her breath again and stood there looking at the man. She was struck dumb by the way he talked.

Then Miss Liza started to teach him how to use his awl and hammer and how to stitch leather.

"Did you teach all these men how to make shoes?" he asked.

Miss Liza tossed her head and stuck out her chin and said, "Are you weak in the head?" And she laughed and ran out of the room.

When dinnertime came, all the men stopped work, took their baskets, and went out into the yard to eat their dinners in the sun—all except the king. He wasn't used to fending for himself, so he had forgotten to bring any dinner. While the others ate, he stayed at his bench and hammered away.

Miss Liza, sitting at the table, asked her daddy who was working when they ought to be eating. "It must be the new man," he said.

She ran and peeped through the door, and sure enough, there was the new man pegging away at some shoes. She went in and asked him why he wasn't eating his dinner with the rest. "Didn't you bring any?"

"No," he said, "I clean forgot it."

"It's a wonder you didn't forget your own head," said Miss Liza.

"That's exactly what I went and did," he said. "That's why

108

I was late this morning; I had to go back home and fetch it."

He looked at her, and she looked at him. And then he laughed, and she began to go red in the face.

"You've got mighty brazen eyes," she said.

"And you've got mighty pretty ones," he replied.

"Don't be impudent," she said.

"A hungry man will say almost anything," he said.

With that she whipped out of the room, and by and by came back with a tray full of vittles. When she set it down on the bench, he took her hand and said, "When I am king, I will make you my queen."

"That's no more than I expect," she said, "for a fortuneteller told me one day that if I was good and quit my behavishness, I would marry high and live well. So I tell you right now I won't marry no shoemaker, because ever since I was born I've been smelling leather and listening to those hammers pound, until it's nearly run me crazy. No, sirree! No shoemaker for me!"

The king ate his dinner slowly and smacked his mouth. "I haven't had such a good dinner since yesterday," he said.

He looked at her, and she looked at him, and this time she burst out laughing. "Whoever and whatever you are, you're no shoemaker," she said. "All the work you have done is totally wrong and will have to be done again. And your hands are soft, and your fingernails are neat and clean."

When she got back into the dining room, she asked her daddy who the new man was. He said, "As far as I know, his name is Bobby Raw."

Next day the new man arrived without any dinner again. Miss Liza told him, "You needn't think I'm going to make any

for you today; you've had time to make your own arrangements."

He said, "In that case I'll have to depend on the king. Maybe he'll be good enough to send me my dinner."

At dinnertime, all the hands went out into the sunshine to eat their meals, but Bobby Raw stayed at his bench, working away, making shoes backward, putting pegs in the wrong place and fixing the heel on the toe, and doing everything that a shoemaker wouldn't do, with no dinner to eat.

Miss Liza said, "The king forgot to send you your dinner, I reckon."

"Give him time, give him time," said the new man.

Miss Liza was blazing mad. She said, "You ain't fit to have no dinner, and this is the last time I'm going to fix you any. I don't see what you come here for anyway. You know very well you couldn't make a shoe if your life depended on it. You haven't been here two days, and already you've caused me more worry than all the other hands put together."

Just then there was a big noise outside, and when Miss Liza looked out there was a coach and four at the door. Servants jumped down from it with dishes of gold and silver, saying, "Dinner for the new hand, with the compliments of the king!"

Well, this set Miss Liza to ruminating. She could see there was some mystery about the new man and the king, but she couldn't see what it was. She asked him, "Why would the king send you your dinner?"

He said, "The king and I are old friends; we've known each other since we were babies. We even sleep in the same bed."

Miss Liza asked him to explain, but he said, "There's only

one way for you to find out the truth, and that is to marry me."

"I won't marry anybody, much less a man who doesn't even know how to make a shoe," she said.

But he courted her, and courted her, and courted her, and by and by she said she would marry him, if only to find out what was between him and the king.

"If you marry me," he said, "you will see as much of the king as you will of me."

They set the wedding day, and that morning the king sent his big gold and silver coach to fetch the couple to the palace. Bobby Raw snuggled by Miss Liza's side, but he didn't say anything. When they came to the palace, there was a great crowd in the streets, cheering and singing; there wasn't standing room for a flea.

Then the couple went into the palace and were married, and then the king led Miss Liza to a great big gold throne with silk and satin all over it, and then she found out that she had married King Bobby the Raw.

And when Miss Liza got used to the house and knew where to hunt for cobwebs, she did her queening as well as any of the rest of them; but King Bobby the Raw never could learn how to make a decent pair of shoes.

RICHMOND HEIGHTS
MEMORIAL LIBRARY
7441 11  AVENUE
RICHMOND HEIGHTS, MO 63117

# NOTES ON THE STORIES

*"Why does he want to spoil a story by telling us what the folklorists think of it? Who cares . . . so long as the story is rolling along on wheels, as you may say?"*

— Joel Chandler Harris, "Miss Liza an' de King"

I hope the following notes will not "spoil the story." Along with the sources of my texts, I have in each case given the relevant Aarne-Thompson international tale type numbers so that those interested in doing so can easily find other versions of the same basic story. For American and English variants, see Ernest W. Baughman, *Type and Motif Index of the Folktales of England and North America*; for international variants, see D. L. Ashliman, *A Guide to Folktales in the English Language*. For an explanation of how the A-T tale types work, and a survey of the international folktale, see Stith Thompson, *The Folktale*. At the end of each note I have summarized the extent of my own involvement in the printed text; this has usually been restricted to minimal editorial work or light retelling, but some texts have caused more problems and have been entirely retold.

N.P.

## A STEPCHILD THAT WAS TREATED MIGHTY BAD

This Kentucky mountain "Snow White" (type 709, *Snow White*) is fairly clearly derived from the Grimm version, until at the end it veers into type 480, *The Kind and Unkind Girls*, a type frequently collected in America and found in its pure form in the story "The Gold in the Chimney."

The story was told by Aunt Lizbeth Fields and printed in Marie Campbell, *Tales from the Cloud Walking Country* (Bloomington: Indiana University Press, 1958). The book contains another fourteen tales from the same teller, who loved especially stories "with all manner of things golden."

Marie Campbell superbly conveys the intimacy of the scene as Aunt Lizbeth Fields recalls and retells the story in her distinctive and compelling voice. I have left in the moments at which she expressed uncertainty about what happened in the story; these are part of the telling. It is interesting that in an American context the royal status of the various characters seems almost irrelevant, while the dwarfs are merely "little men," and the magical speaking mirror becomes simply a reflector of the stepmother's own vanity and mean-heartedness. The magical element of the story is subordinated to the moral.

Reprinted without change.

## THE TWO WITCHES

This story is taken from Helen Zunser, "A New Mexican Village," *Journal of American Folk-Lore*, vol. 48, 1935. It was told by Antonio Lorenz, a blacksmith in Hot Springs, New Mexico, and is a version of type 325, *The Magician and His Pupil*.

The story has been completely retold, and I have given it a new ending. The original ending is unsatisfactory; it forgets all about the princess and instead visits a violent death on the coyote.

## LADY FEATHERFLIGHT

This lovely long tale is a version of one of the most widely distributed of all folktales, type 313, *The Girl as Helper in the Hero's Flight*. There are quite a number of American versions, and this tale type is notable as the fairy tale most often told by African American narrators, who were perhaps attracted to its theme of escape from an overbearing master; a good African American version is "Jack Beats the Devil" in Roger D. Abrahams, *Afro-American Folktales*.

"Lady Featherflight," however, is clearly of British origin. It was discussed by William Wells Newell at the International Folk-Lore Congress of 1891 and printed in the *Papers and Transactions* of the Congress edited by Joseph Jacobs and Alfred Nutt (London: David Nutt, 1892); it was also printed in vol. 6 of the *Journal of American Folk-*

*Lore*. Newell collected it from Mrs. J. B. Warner of Cambridge, Massachusetts, who had heard it from her aunt, Miss Elizabeth Hoar, of Concord, Massachusetts, in whose family "it has been traditional."

Here was a case of a traditional fairy tale gathered not from the lips of an unlettered peasant but from a family of social standing—proof that folktales were also the property of the educated. It is quite likely, though, that the story entered the family tradition via a nursemaid, and there is some evidence that the end of the story was rather effectively tidied up for the nursery.

Lightly retold.

# NO ESTIENDO

Joke tales such as this are told in every country, and even they have their Aarne-Thompson tale type number: 1699, *Misunderstanding Because of Ignorance of a Foreign Language*.

This delicately judged example was contributed by folklorist Américo Paredes to Richard M. Dorson, *Buying the Wind: Regional Folklore in the United States* (Chicago & London: University of Chicago Press, 1964); Paredes heard it from his cousin Ignacio Mansano in 1926.

Reprinted without change.

# KING PEACOCK

This French Creole tale was collected from an African American storyteller (described as "an old negro from la Vacherie") and published in Alcée Fortier, *Louisiana Folk-Tales* (Boston & New York: Published for the American Folk-Lore Society by Houghton, Mifflin and Company, 1895). It is essentially another version of type 709, *Snow White*, though so different in flavor from "A Stepchild That Was Treated Mighty Bad" that it turns into a completely different story. There are also elements of type 425, *The Search for the Lost Husband*.

It is a strange, dreamlike tale, with the peacock, and then the peacock feathers, leading the girl on to meet her true love, King Peacock. The storyteller does not trouble to exact retribution on the evil mother, or to draw a link between the fine gentleman whom the mother rejects and King Peacock; nor do we ever find out what the girl does with the third seed. Yet no more is needed to produce a haunting tale.

The story is evidently of French origin, though I do not know of an exact parallel in French tradition. I have completely revised Fortier's English text against the Creole original.

## COLD FEET AND THE LONESOME QUEEN

This tale from Marie Campbell, *Tales from the Cloud Walking Country*, was one of "a fine mort of olden tales" recorded from the ballad singer Big Nelt. Many of his Celtic-derived tales were learned from his mother; others, like this one, from "the Irishman" who stayed with his family for several weeks when Nelt was young. In 1933, Big Nelt was around sixty years old, so he had remembered the Irishman's stories all his adult life. He may have been particularly attracted to this one because he himself was rather like Cold Feet in size and demeanor. Marie Campbell was told, "Iffen you meet up with him, you can know Big Nelt on account of him being so big and high and not wearing no shoes but in chilling weather."

The story closely parallels the tale "Cold Feet and the Queen of Lonesome Island" in Jeremiah Curtin, *Hero Tales of Ireland* (Boston: Little, Brown, and Co., 1894). Verbal echoes suggest that the Irishman learned the story from Curtin's version, probably as first printed in the Sunday supplement of the New York *Sun*. It is a version of type 304, *The Hunter*, with the added tall-tale motif of the child's supernatural growth, strength, and appetite.

Reprinted with no change, save for the omission where indicated on p. 54 of a total of seventeen words relating to Cold Feet's unorthodox courtship of the Lonesome Queen.

## THE FRIENDLY DEMON

From Arthur Huff Fauset, "Negro Folk Tales from the South," *Journal of American Folk-Lore*, vol. 40, 1927. This tale was collected from Allan Coates, aged twenty-eight, a veteran of the First World War, in the Government Hospital, Tuskegee, Alabama. It combines two tale types: 561, *Aladdin*, and 571, *Making the Princess Laugh*.

The original text is rather muddled, and I have retold it completely; I have tried to retain some of the sense of the storyteller's voice, especially the rhythmic insistence with which Allan Coates punctuated his narrative with the word "see."

## THE LITTLE BULL WITH THE GOLDEN HORNS

This is one of a group of French wonder tales that survived in the oral tradition of the Old Mines area of Missouri. It was told by Frank Bourisaw to Joseph Médard Carrière and published by him in *Tales from the French Folk-Lore of Missouri* (Evanston & Chicago: Northwestern University, 1937).

Frank "Boy" Bourisaw was one of several local storytellers or *conteurs* renowned and respected for their skill. One person told Rosemary Hyde Thomas, "We'd sit down at seven or eight o'clock, and he could tell stories that would go on until five o'clock the next morning. He'd just keep on telling all different ones."

This particular story starts out with a simple tale about tricking a dull-witted devil or ogre, type 1030, *The Crop Division*. It then keeps the amusement going by opening out into a longer fairy tale, which is a kind of mixture of type 328, *The Boy Steals the Giant's Treasure*, and type 1525, *The Master Thief*.

One interesting feature of this narrative is the glimmer of a suggestion that Big Devil and his wife are actually Little John's parents; they are referred to as *L'vieux* and *La vieille*, "the old man" and "the old woman," the same terms used to refer to the parents in the first sentence. Little John then goes to live with the king and queen, who show a parental concern for him while his attitude to them is that of a rebellious teenager. Little John's restless discontent is so well drawn that I have allowed myself the liberty of adding one last sentence to my version. The original ends with Big Devil trapped for good in the iron coach, but I cannot believe that Little John would be either so heartless or so constant as to keep him prisoner forever. Big Devil is not, I think, intended to be *the* Devil; he is the archetypal stupid giant.

The text is retranslated from the French, a task made feasible by the opportunity to refer to the version by Rosemary Hyde Thomas in her excellent selection of Carrière's tales, *It's Good to Tell You* (1981). The names of the characters are "P'tsit Jean" and "Grand Guiab'." In a Canadian version, "Le Boeuf à cornes d'or" in S. Marie-Ursule, *Civilisation traditionelle des Lavalois* (Quebec, 1951), the hero is Tit-Jean.


# THE GOLD IN THE CHIMNEY


This little tale, a version of type 480, *The Kind and Unkind Girls*, has been very frequently collected in the United States, and is also one of the most commonly found in England (see "The Old Witch" in Neil Philip, *The Penguin Book of English Folktales*). The similarity of the rhymes in the American and English texts shows that most American versions derive from English tradition, although it has also been recorded from Italian and French sources. This one comes from Leonard W. Roberts, "The Cante Fable in Eastern Kentucky," *Midwest Folklore*, vol. 6, 1956; another version collected by Roberts, also entitled "The Gold in the Chimley," can be found in his *South from Hell-fer-Sartin*.

Another notable American version, "The Three Brothers and the Hag" (*Journal of American Folk-Lore*, vol. 8, 1895) is unusual in having boys instead of girls, so the hag sings:

> Have you seen a boy
> With a wig, with a wag,
> With a long leather bag,
> Who stole all the money
> Ever I had?

I have made a few minor adjustments to the source text (for instance, changing "chimley" to "chimney").

## THREE EILESCHPIJJEL STORIES

These Pennsylvania Dutch stories of the crafty fool Eileschpijjel (pronounced "Eye-laschpiggel" with a hard "g") come from Thomas R. Brendle and William S. Troxell, *Pennsylvania German Folk Tales, Legends, Once-Upon-a-Time Stories, Maxims and Sayings* (Norristown, Pa.: Pennsylvania German Society, *Proceedings*, vol. 50, 1944). Eilesch-pijjel is a very popular character in Pennsylvania Dutch folklore, whose idiocy shades into cleverness. These three typical stories show him working in the rural setting of the storytellers themselves.

Eileschpijjel is known in German and Belgian tradition as Till Eulenspiegel ("Fool Owlglass"), whose stories were recorded and amplified by the Belgian writer Charles de Coster. In de Coster's work, Eulenspiegel has more of the malicious trickster in his personality, and less of the lovable fool.

"The Wagon Load" is type 1242, *Loading the Wood.*

The texts are reprinted with only minor changes.

## JACK AND THE BEANSTALK

This lively Kentucky version of "Jack and the Beanstalk" comes from Leonard W. Roberts, *Old Greasybeard: Tales from the Cumberland Gap* (Detroit: Folklore Associates, 1969). It was collected by Mrs. Flora Mae Hicks in 1954 from "an old story-telling man," Oscar Cotton, then aged ninety-seven.

The international tale type 328, *The Boy Steals the Giant's Treasure*, features the beanstalk motif only in English or English-derived versions. Oddly enough, although "Jack and Beanstalk" is the best known of all English folktales, no oral version has ever been recorded from the mainstream English tradition, where it is known from a skit of c. 1730 and chapbook printings c. 1807. The only oral texts are two very wayward and idiosyncratic Gypsy versions collected by T. W. Thompson. The standard "English" text is that of Joseph Jacobs (see Neil Philip, *The Penguin Book of English Folktales*), but this was actually a reconstruction of a version told to him as a child in Australia.

Therefore, the American versions of "Jack and the Beanstalk" are of particular importance. This one, for instance, with its insistence that Jack was merely recovering his own property rather than stealing, echoes a feature of the 1807 chapbook text that Joseph Jacobs dismissed as moralizing interference from the editor. The rhymes are also very interesting. The sequence of Jack's "bargains" is very like that in a folksong or nursery rhyme, "My father died, but I can't tell you how," in which Jack the plowboy inherits six horses. He sells the horses and buys a cow, sells the cow and buys a calf, sells the calf and buys a cat, and then:

> I sold my cat, and bought me a mouse;
> He carried fire in his tail, and burnt down my house:
>> With my wing wang waddle oh,
>> Jack sing saddle oh,
>> Blowsey boys bubble oh,
>> Under the broom.

This succession of daft bargains is also known as a folktale, type 1415, *Lucky Hans*. An American version, "Setting Down the Budget," can be found in Vance Randolph, *The Devil's Pretty Daughter*.

A storyteller interviewed by Henry Mayhew in a London workhouse in 1861 told him, "The best man in the story is always called Jack." This simple fact enables us to trace the English fairy tale tradition with some confidence in its Appalachian flowering, first recorded by Richard Chase in his book *The Jack Tales*.

I have made only minor modifications to the text, with one slightly cheeky addition: the beautiful American detail of Jack's disguise as a paperboy actually comes from one of the other American versions, narrated by Mary Smith of Lincoln, Pennsylvania, and printed in Elsie Clews Parsons, "Tales from Maryland and Pennsylvania," *Journal of American Folk-Lore*, vol. 30, 1917. Others can be found in Chase, *The Jack Tales*, and in Isabel Gordon Carter, "Mountain White Folk-Lore: Tales from the Southern Blue Ridge," *Journal of American Folk-Lore*, vol. 38, 1925. In a variant, "The Big Old Giant," in Vance Randolph, *Who Blew Up the Church House?* the beanstalk is replaced by a cornstalk.

## THE BIG CABBAGE

This short lying contest (type 1920A) comes from Richard Dorson, *Negro Tales from Pine Bluff, Arkansas, and Calvin, Michigan* (Bloomington: Indiana University Press, 1958), and was recorded in Calvin, Michigan, from an African American storyteller. The motif of "the great cabbage" is one of many such traditional boasts; an English folktale attributes the boast about the giant vegetable to Mark Twain, in his capacity as a teller of tall tales ("Mark Twain in the Fens," in Katharine Briggs, *A Dictionary of British Folk-Tales*). A similar tale, "The Turnip," can be found in Elsie Clews Parsons, "Tales from Guilford County," *Journal of American Folk-Lore*, vol. 30, 1917.

A short story "Preacher Tells a Lie" in John A. Burrison, *Storytellers: Folktales and Legends from the South*, recorded in 1979 from another African American storyteller, Hattie Mae Dawson of Atlanta, tells how three boys held a lying contest, with a dog as the prize for the teller of "the biggest story." The preacher happens along and chides them, saying, "Sha-a-ame, sha-a-ame. Why, I never tol' a lie in my life." One of the boys jumps up, shouting, "Give 'im the dog!" The same story is told in Westmorland, England, about the Bishop of Carlisle (Neil Philip, *The Penguin Book of English Folktales*, introduction).

Reprinted without change.

## TOBE KILLED A BEAR

This story was told by Pete Woolsey, Pineville, Missouri, in September 1924, and printed by the great Ozark folklorist Vance Randolph in his *Sticks in the Knapsack and*

*Other Ozark Folk Tales* (New York: Columbia University Press, 1958). It is, as Ernest W. Baughman says in his notes to Randolph's volume, "a wonderfully Americanized form of part of the Beowulf story."

The Old English poem "Beowulf" survives in a single tenth-century manuscript, the record of a poem that had survived in oral tradition for at least two hundred years before that. In one of its major scenes, the hero Beowulf confronts a monster that has been attacking the king's hall and tears off its arm with his bare hands. To find this story line still surviving in oral tradition in the Ozarks in the twentieth century, as a tall tale attached to a legendary local strong man, is quite extraordinary. Baughman lists a number of striking similarities between the two stories, including the hanging up of the torn-off limb. He also points out that the name Beowulf ("Bee-hunter") means "bear."

I have made only minor changes to the text.

## THE CAT THAT WENT A-TRAVELING

This is another Kentucky mountain story from Marie Campbell, *Tales from the Cloud Walking Country*. It was told by a Regular Baptist preacher, Uncle Blessing. It is a version of type 130, *The Animals in Night Quarters*, best known as the Grimms' "The Musicians of Bremen."

The version is quite close to a Scottish tale from J. F. Campbell's *Popular Tales of the West Highlands* (Edinburgh: Edmonston and Douglas, 1860), "The White Pet," suggesting a possible Scottish origin.

Reprinted without change.

## THE ENCHANTED PRINCE

This magical fairy tale was collected in New Mexico by the great folklorist Aurelio M. Espinosa in the 1930s and is taken from *The Folklore of Spain in the American Southwest* (Norman and London: University of Oklahoma Press, 1985), edited by his son J. Manuel Espinosa. It is a version of a widely distributed European tale, type 432, *The Prince as a Bird*, which is found both in native Spanish tradition and in the Spanish-speaking New World. Versions from Mexico and Chile do not contain the "One Eye, Two Eyes, Three Eyes" motif, which usually opens a variant type of the Cinderella story. That the envious mother and sisters, hoping to inherit the Green Bird's magnificent castle, find only an empty desert is a particularly New Mexican touch.

Text lightly amended.

# MISS LIZA AND THE KING

I found this story in a little-known children's book by Joel Chandler Harris, *Wally Wanderoon and His Storytelling Machine* (New York: Mclure, Phillips & Co., 1902), where he puts it in the mouth of an African American girl, Drusilla, and describes it as a tale "which for many years had been popular with negro girls between the ages of twelve and twenty." It is one of those tales which, because he detected a European origin, Harris was reluctant to put in his *Uncle Remus* books. He is surely right in this instance to say that Bobby de Raw is a corruption of Robert le Roi, suggesting a French origin. But this is unlike any French folktale I know; nor does it fit neatly into any international tale type.

There is perhaps an echo of type 844, *The Luck-bringing Shirt*, in some versions of which a dissatisfied king is told he will only be content when he wears the shoes of a happy man. He goes all over the kingdom searching for such a man – but the only truly happy man he finds has no shoes! There is also a resemblance to type 951, *The King and the Robber*, in which a king goes in disguise to learn how the poor live and falls in with a gang of robbers who are planning to rob the royal treasury; when they are caught, they recognize the king as their former comrade, and he pardons them. But perhaps the closest parallel is type 900, *King Thrushbeard*, in which a princess is punished for her haughtiness by being married off to a beggar, who reveals himself only at the end of the story as *King Thrushbeard*. A good version of this can be found in Grimms' *Fairy Tales*, and an American version is "Old Bushy Beard" in Marie Campbell, *Tales from the Cloud Walking Country*.

In "Miss Liza and the King" a specifically American attitude can be seen adapting and revising traditional folktales to suit a new a country and a new consciousness. The way in which the king is regarded as less worthy of respect than a man who does honest work with his hands reminds me of one of the best American literary fairy tales, Frank Stockton's "The Banished King," first published in *St. Nicholas* in 1882 (collected in *The Fairy Tales of Frank Stockton*). In this tale the king of "a kingdom in which everything seemed to go wrong" is banished for a year to find out how other countries are governed. When he returns, he finds everything running smoothly under the queen's rule, and "it was not long before he came to the conclusion that the main thing which had been wrong in his kingdom was himself." He decides to give up being a king, as "he would get on much better in some other business or profession." While there is no suggestion that Stockton's tale influenced Harris's, it is interesting to find the same motif of the king who needs something better to do with his time in both an oral and a written American fairy tale.

Retold; dialect and phonetic spelling regularized.

# FURTHER READING

*For sources of the individual stories, see the Notes.*

Aarne, Antti. *The Types of the Folktale*. Translated and enlarged by Stith Thompson, 2nd revision. Helsinki: Suomalainen Tiedeakatemia, 1961.

Abrahams, Roger D. *Afro-American Folktales*. New York: Pantheon Books, 1985.

Ashliman, D. L. *A Guide to Folktales in the English Language, Based on the Aarne-Thompson Classification System*. New York; Westport, Connecticut; London: Greenwood Press, 1987.

Bascom, William. *African Folktales in the New World*. Bloomington & Indianapolis: Indiana University Press, 1992.

Baughman, Ernest W. *Type and Motif Index of the Folk-Tales of England and North America*. The Hague: Mouton & Co., 1966.

Boggs, Ralph S. "North Carolina Folktales Current in the 1820's," and "North Carolina White Folktales and Riddles." *Journal of American Folk-Lore*, vol. 47, 1934.

Botkin, B. A. *A Treasury of American Folklore: Stories, Ballads, and Traditions of the People*. New York: Crown Publishers, 1944.

Briggs, Katharine M. *A Dictionary of British Folktales in the English Language*. London: Routledge & Kegan Paul, 1970-71.

Brunvand, Jan Harold. *American Folklore: An Encyclopedia*. New York & London: Garland Publishing, 1996.

Burrison, John A. *Storytellers: Folktales and Legends from the South*. Athens & London: University of Georgia Press, 1989.

Campbell, Marie. *Tales from the Cloud Walking Country*. Bloomington: Indiana University Press, 1958.

Carter, Isabel Gordon. "Mountain White Folk-Lore: Tales from the Southern Blue Ridge." *Journal of American Folk-Lore*, vol. 38, 1925.

Chase, Richard. *The Jack Tales*. Boston: Houghton Mifflin Company, 1943.

———. *Grandfather Tales*. Boston: Houghton Mifflin Company, 1948.

———. *American Folk Tales and Songs*. New York: Dover Publications, Inc., 1971 (first published 1956).

Coffin, Tristram Potter & Cohen, Hennig. *Folklore in America*. New York: Doubleday, 1966.

———. *Folklore from the Working Folk of America*. New York: Anchor Press/Doubleday, 1973.

Cohn, Amy. *From Sea to Shining Sea: A Treasury of American Folklore and Folk Songs.* New York: Scholastic, Inc., 1993.

Dorson, Richard M. *American Folklore.* Chicago & London: The University of Chicago Press, 1959.

―――. *Buying the Wind: Regional Folklore in the United States.* Chicago & London: The University of Chicago Press, 1964.

―――. *Handbook of American Folklore.* Bloomington: Indiana University Press, 1983.

Espinosa, J. Manuel. *Spanish Folk Tales from New Mexico.* New York: G. E. Stechert and Co., 1937.

Glazer, Mark. *Flour from Another Sack.* Edinburg, Tx.: Pan American University, 1982.

Hamilton, Virginia. *The People Could Fly: American Black Folktales.* New York: Alfred A. Knopf, 1985.

Harris, Joel Chandler. *The Complete Tales of Uncle Remus.* Compiled by Richard Chase. Boston: Houghton Mifflin Company, 1955.

Haywood, Charles. *A Bibliography of North American Folklore and Folksong.* 2nd rev. ed. New York: Dover Publications, 1961.

Matthias, Elizabeth & Raspa, Richard. *Italian Folktales in America.* Detroit: Wayne State University Press, 1985.

Miller, Elaine K. *Mexican Folk Narrative from the Los Angeles Area.* Austin & London: University of Texas Press, 1973.

Osborne, Mary Pope. *American Tall Tales.* New York: Alfred A. Knopf, 1991.

Parsons, Elsie Clews. "Tales from Guilford County, North Carolina," and "Tales from Maryland and Pennsylvania." *Journal of American Folk-Lore,* vol. 30, 1917.

―――. *Folk-Lore from the Cape Verde Islands.* Cambridge, Mass.: The American Folk-Lore Society, 1923.

Philip, Neil. *The Penguin Book of English Folktales.* London: Penguin Books, 1992.

―――. *American Fairy Tales.* New York: Hyperion, 1996.

Randolph, Vance. *Who Blowed Up the Church House? and Other Ozark Folk Tales.* New York: Columbia University Press, 1952.

―――. *The Devil's Pretty Daughter and Other Ozark Folk Tales.* New York: Columbia University Press, 1955.

Roberts, Leonard W. *South from Hell-fer-Sartin: Kentucky Mountain Folk Tales.* Lexington: The University of Kentucky Press, 1955.

Stockton, Frank. *The Fairy Tales of Frank Stockton.* Edited by Jack Zipes. New York: Signet, 1990.

Thomas, Rosemary Hyde. *It's Good to Tell You: French Folktales from Missouri.* Columbia & London: University of Missouri Press, 1981.

Thompson, Stith. *The Folktale.* New York: Holt, Rinehart & Winston, 1946.

―――. *Tales of the North American Indians.* Bloomington: Indiana University Press, 1966 (first published 1929).

Villa, Susie Hoogasian. *100 Armenian Folktales and Their Folkloristic Relevance.* Detroit: Wayne State University Press, 1966.

Zumwalt, Rosemary Lévy. *American Folklore Scholarship.* Bloomington & Indianapolis: Indiana University Press, 1988.

# ACKNOWLEDGMENTS

The author is grateful to all the storytellers and collectors who have lent a feather to thatch this barn. The author and the publisher would like to thank the following copyright holders for permission to reprint and retell the stories listed below. Every effort has been made to contact copyright holders, but we would be interested to hear from any copyright holders not here acknowledged.

"A Stepchild That Was Treated Mighty Bad," "Cold Feet and the Lonesome Queen," and "The Cat That Went a-Traveling" copyright © 1958 by Indiana University Press, reprinted from Marie Campbell, *Tales from the Cloud Walking Country*, by permission of Indiana University Press; "The Two Witches," from Helen Zunser, "A New Mexican Village," reproduced by permission of the American Folklore Society from, *Journal of American Folklore*, volume 48:3, 1935. Not for further reproduction; "No Estiendo" copyright © 1964 by the University of Chicago, reprinted from Richard M. Dorson *Buying the Wind*, by permission of the University of Chicago Press; "King Peacock" from Alcée Fortier, *Louisiana Folk-Tales*, new translation copyright © 1999 by Neil Philip; "The Friendly Demon" from Arthur Huff Fauset, "Negro Folk Tales from the South," reproduced by permission of the American Folklore Society from *Journal of American Folklore*, volume 40:157, 1927. Not for further reproduction; "The Little Bull with the Golden Horns" (*Le p'tsit boeu[f] au cornes d'or*) in Joseph Médard Carrière, *Tales from the French Folk-Lore of Missouri*, copyright © 1937 by Northwestern University Studies, printed and translated by permission of Northwestern University Press, translation copyright © 1999 by Neil Philip; "The Gold in the Chimney" from Leonard W. Roberts, "The Cante Fable in Eastern Kentucky," in *Midwest Folklore*, vol. 6, 1956, reprinted by permission of Mrs. Edith R. Roberts; "Three Eileschpijjel Stories" from Thomas R. Brendle and William S. Troxell *Pennsylvania German Folk Tales*, 1944, reprinted by permission of the Pennsylvania German Society; "Jack and the Beanstalk" copyright © 1969 by Folklore Associates, Inc., reprinted from Leonard W. Roberts, *Old Greasybeard*, by permission of Mrs. Edith R. Roberts; "The Big Cabbage" copyright © 1958 by Indiana University Press, reprinted from Richard M. Dorson, *Negro Tales from Pine Bluff, Arkansas, and Calvin, Michigan*, by permission of Indiana University Press; "Tobe Killed a Bear" from *Sticks in the Knapsack and Other Ozark Folk Tales*, Vance Randolph © 1958, Columbia University Press. Reprinted with the permission of the publisher; "The Enchanted Prince" adapted from "The Enchanted Prince" in *The Folklore of Spain in the American Southwest*, by Aurelio M. Espinosa, edited by J. Manuel Espinosa, pp. 191–195. Copyright © 1985 by the University of Oklahoma Press, Norman.